Forced, Filthy & Rough Forbidden& Erotic BDSM Sex Stories Collection:

Erotica For Women- Submission, Femdom, CNC, Spanking, Domination, Role-Play, First Time Anal, Gangbangs& More

Written By:
G.G. Goode

Goode Publications

Table of Contents

Marie's Master

Marie went through her day absent-mindedly. It was a Friday, the last day of the work week and she couldn't wait for the weekend. She loved her job, usually, but today was one of those days. All throughout the day, she had something completely different on her mind. But she just had a few hours left until she could do it. Marie was the legal secretary to one of the biggest lawyers in the city. Her job consisted of him demanding coffee almost every hour on the dot, proofreading legal documents, scheduling appointments, keeping his calendar up to date, and various other personal issues he needed fixed. Although her boss could be difficult, it was also fulfilling at times. There was just something about keeping his life in order and making sure everything was perfect, that made her feel like her own was just fine.

Outside of work, she was a mess. She dressed the part of a high-end person, an upper-class woman that had her fiery red hair neatly pinned up. A woman who wore form fitting dress suits that showed off her figure. A woman who could coordinate fifteen meetings over a five-day week as well as business dinners.

On the contrary, though, she was the complete opposite person of who she fronted as in the professional capacity. Marie was actually a simple girl in her personal life, and she had one deep, dark secret that she couldn't allow anyone in her workplace to know about. Every single Friday evening, at 9pm, she would go to a club that promoted sexuality and fun.

It was called Hot Red and she was introduced to it by a good friend almost exactly a year ago. Her friend, Angela, suggested this kink club to Marie because she was lonely and regular, ordinary one-night stands weren't doing it for her anymore. Marie wasn't really looking for anything serious. She was twenty-five years old and a career woman, she didn't see herself finding the time for finding a man. Just the thought of it made her feel anxious – who knew how many men would waste her time and end up breaking her heart? She preferred to rather be alone than deal with all the potential problems that came with trying to find the love of her life. She just *knew* that her dedication to her career and her independence would be an issue to most men if she tried dating. It was hopeless.

So, The Hot Red Club was the perfect thing for her. She stared at the time on her desktop until the time ticked over for the end of her workday. She immediately began packing her stuff up. It was the same every Friday. The Hot Red was seemingly the only thing she enjoyed anymore and when the day for it came, it was the only thing she could think about. She shut down her computer and got ready to leave. Marie made sure she had everything and got a fright when she looked up and saw Angela standing in front of her, next to her desk.

She was a tall woman with silky white blonde hair, cut in a bob. Angela and Marie went way back, they knew each other since they were in high school. They instantly connected and they worked together in the same office due to their close connection, although Angela was in a different department – she worked as an associate. She had just finished her law degree about a year ago and was working her way up in the field. They were inseparable. They even lived a five-minute walk away from each other. The sly smile on her face showed that she knew where Marie was going in a few hours. It made Marie blush. They were close but Marie was different to Angela, she didn't like people knowing the specifics of her sex life.

"Hey, babe. Where ya going? What are you in such a rush for?" Angela asked.

"You're being disingenuous. You know *exactly* where I'm going!" Marie said, "Now shush. I'll see you tomorrow."

"No, I don't know where you're going, what are you talking about?" Angela said with tongue in cheek.

"Shh. Stop it. You always tease me about it. I'm going to The Hot Red today. There, I said it. Are you happy?" Marie whispered. She looped her bag over her head so the strap lay diagonally across her chest.

"I just wanted you to say. I love seeing you all flustered," Angela said, "You think you're gonna be seein' that hunk again, hmm?"

Marie's boss walked past them and tipped his hat to say goodbye for the week. Angela said goodbye to him. When he was gone, Marie let out a sigh.

"The workplace is not the time for this, Angie. Mark literally just walked past, and he could have heard you," Marie said, flustered, "But yes. He's been there every Friday to see me since those first few weeks I started coming to the club. So, he will definitely be there today."

As frustrating as her best friend was, she loved her to bits at the end of the day.

"Hmm, I really wish I could meet this guy. He sounds like a real hunk," Angela said. Most of the people were out of the office by now, so they could talk freely.

"It's just sex, Angie. It's not like we're in a relationship," Marie said.

"Oh, really? You've never fucked anyone else at the club except for that one girl, that one time, other than that, you only fuck him. It sounds pretty exclusive to me, anyway. Besides, I love the whole mysterious, broody vibe he gives off. Maybe you two can become official someday."

Angela winked at Marie. Marie sighed.

"You're such a hopeless romantic, babe. I know you're just trying to make me uncomfortable because for some reason, you find that fun. Come on, I'll walk you home," Marie said.

They made their way out of the office and walked together. Angela looped her arm in Marie's as they walked. Their relationship was so close that they could be mistaken for being in a relationship. There is just something special about a best friend relationship between two girls, though, they cuddled and shared a bed without judgment. They told each other everything. But Marie especially loved her best friend because they were polar opposites. Angela was tall and blonde and bubbly, whereas Marie was shorter, a little more curvy and more introverted than her.

Marie stopped in front of Angela's apartment and they went inside. Marie sat down at the small kitchen island as Angela pulled out two glasses and a bottle of wine.

"I hope you have fun later today, babe. I'm so happy you found something that keeps you satisfied. I can't wait to hear about what you get up to today," Angela said.

"Sometimes I wonder if you just like hearing about the juicy details because it turns you on. Besides, I always have fun. How couldn't I, when in a BDSM club?" Marie giggled.

"Okay true. And so what if it does? I should really try it sometime. It's just so daunting to go alone, ya know?"

"What happened to my brave and strong best friend? Since when are you scared to do anything involving being around people?"

"Well, it's different when sex is involved. I'm a little more nervous about it," Angela said. She tucked a tuft of hair behind her ear.

"Well – if you ever want to, you know, try it, you could come with me some time?"

"What? Are you serious? I don't want to impose... and I mean, would you even be comfortable with a threesome? You're very...territorial over Alex," Angela said.

"Oh! I wasn't actually thinking of a threesome when I mentioned bringing you along, but if you want to... I wouldn't uh, be against it. As long as you're the submissive kind, you'd fit in perfectly."

"Well, babe, we've made out so many times when we were drunk that I'm not shy about being naked in front of you... I've always wanted to say this to you, but it was never the right time. But you're pretty fuckin' hot. I'd definitely do you. Problem is, though, I'm very much a dominant type."

"Oh! Uh, oh my god. Okay. Thank you, Angie. Maybe I'll speak to Alex and see what he thinks," Marie said.

Angela bit her lip. "What would you think about being dominated by two people? Alex and I could work together on our little submissive slut."

Marie shifted in her seat and felt an intense hotness in her panties. She was sure that she was wet just thinking about it.

"Angie – that actually sounds incredible. I will need to ask his permission first, though, since he's my dom and all, but I'll let you know. I would actually love that. Come to think of it, that's my ultimate fantasy."

"I'm so glad you're on board for it. If he says yes – oh man, I'll be so happy. Look, I know we're best friends and despite us kissing and all that, are you sure you'd be one hundred percent on board for it? Like, it won't affect our friendship or anything like that?"

"Not at all. I don't think it would change a thing. Honestly, I think it would bring us closer together. Was this your plan all along? You know, since introducing me to the club?"

"No, not really. I mean, I have thought about it but I was too scared to say it in case you said no. I wouldn't want to make things awkward."

Marie sipped on her wine and looked her best friend in the eye. Before Marie could react, she was pinned down on the kitchen island and Angela was sitting on her lap, holding Marie's hands above her head.

Marie was soaking wet now.

Angela was significantly bigger in overall size and stronger than Marie, so being pinned down by her meant she couldn't move an inch.

"I couldn't wait any more," Angela whispered in her ear, "You're just so fucking sexy."

Angela planted kisses up Marie's neck. Marie breathed heavily and let out a moan when Angela nibbled on her ear – her ultimate weak spot. The sensation of having her hands held so tightly and not being able to move sent Marie into a spiral.

"Think of this as a test for next time," Angela whispered.

She planted her lips on Marie's and she whimpered. Every single inch of Marie's body was ebbing with pleasure even though they hadn't even gone that far yet. Was she always attracted to her best friend all along? There was just something about kissing a woman that could never compare to kissing a man – Angela's lips were soft, and she tasted sweet. There was no stubble to scratch her face. She could smell her flowery perfume and felt like she could sniff that and only that for the rest of eternity.

Angela let go of one of Marie's hands and held both of her wrists in one. Angela slowly unbuttoned Marie's white shirt, her breasts bursting out once they were released from the pressure of the thin fabric.

"No bra, huh?" Angela said, "Such a naughty, naughty girl."

"Bras are uncomfortable," Marie said softly.

"You should go braless more often, your tits are glorious," Angela said.

Before Marie could reply, Angela dove her face into her breasts, planting kisses on her supple flesh and occasional nibbles as she came closer and closer to her nipples. Her bites were not as gentle as her kisses were, but Marie loved it anyway. Something about mixing pain and pleasure made it all the more enjoyable.

Angela's hands slowly trailed down Marie's body, she counted the inches as she came closer and closer to her wetness. Angela reached Marie's inner thighs, her long nails tickling her as she went. She lifted up Marie's knee length skirt and looked down in delight. She let go of Marie's wrists and fully lifted her skirt up to her waist. With great force, she ripped her pantyhose apart so she could touch her panties. Angela didn't hesitate to rub her clit through her panties. Marie wore a pair of plain white cotton panties, her wetness making them sheer and showing off her plump labia.

With two fingers, Angela stroked up and down the lips of Marie's tingling cunt, pressing down on her clit and making circular motions. Marie let out a soft moan each time Angela touched her hole and then her clit. Angela had a pleased smile on her face the entire time. With her other hand, she played with Marie's ample breasts, taking her nipple between two fingers and pinching softly. Angela looked Marie in the eyes and nodded, as if to ask if she could go any further. Marie nodded back enthusiastically. She couldn't wait any more.

"Would you be a good girl and tell me when you are close to cumming?" Angela said seductively.

"Mhm-mm. Yes," Marie whimpered.

"Yes what?"

"Yes, mistress," Marie said.

Angela bit her lip and smiled again.

"Good girl."

Angela slipped her fingers underneath the waistband of Marie's panties and slowly inched herself lower and lower. Again, it felt like an eternity before she touched her where she wanted it.

Expert fingers rubbed her clit then stopped each time she felt she was almost close, to her surprise, Angela shoved two fingers inside of her, slowly pumping in and out of her before increasing the pace. With her thumb, she rubbed her clit as she fingered Marie. She felt an intense pressure building up inside of her, knowing she couldn't take it anymore.

"I'm gonna cum," Marie moaned.

"Good girl," Angela whispered.

The touch stopped abruptly to Marie's disappointment. She pulled her fingers out of her and shoved them in her mouth. Like the *good girl* she was, Marie lapped up her own creamy juices off of Angela's fingers.

Angela pulled her own panties off then mounted Marie, scooting upwards to Marie's face. Angela pulled her skirt up and out of the way and gripped Marie's hair tightly, lifting up her head.

"You're only allowed to come once I am satisfied," Angela said.

"Yes, mistress," Marie said.

She admired Angela's neatly trimmed pussy. Her pink lips were inviting, and she dove into her cunt without hesitation. Angela's moans came in no time and it filled Marie with an intense determination to make her best friend cum. Marie's tongue flicked at Angela's clit, alternating between that and suckling on it lightly. She noticed that Angela especially liked it when she flicked at her clit with her tongue with great intensity, so she kept that up. She continued with that and Angela's back arched, her thighs tightening around Marie's face.

Angela rested her hands on Marie's breasts and her grip tightened more and more as she came closer and closer to climax. Marie felt Angela's thighs uncontrollably shaking so she kept up with what she was doing and didn't stop until she reached climax.

"Oh my god, I'm gonna cum," Angela said through her moans.

Marie lapped up her juices as she convulsed and tensed and had her final release.

"Angela," Marie said, catching her breath, "That was incredible."

"You're so good at this," Angela said. She was practically panting, trying to catch her breath again.

"What can I say?" Marie giggled, "I'm good at giving pleasure."

"Yes, you are," Angela said. She reached down and kissed Marie on the lips, tasting her own juices in the process.

Marie checked her watch and saw what time it was. "Ah, dammit. I have to get ready for the club. Can we continue this at a later date?" Marie said.

"Aw, now I feel bad that I couldn't finish you off," Angela sulked.

"You don't have to, I love being denied an orgasm. So, it's a win-win," Marie said with a wink.

"Okay. I'll see you for brunch tomorrow?"

"Of course, it's tradition at this point."

Marie made her way back home. She had already laid her outfit out in the morning before she went to work. Just how her dom liked it: white knee length socks, a short red plaid skirt and a thin white button up shirt. She pulled it all on and double checked how she looked in the mirror with a spin. As always, she looked amazing. She unpinned her red locks and tied them up into a high ponytail instead. Lastly, she pulled on a long black coat so that she didn't turn any heads as she walked to the club. She buttoned it up and did one last thing: a beautiful red lipstick the color of blood.

She didn't need to bring anything with her, so she set off on her walk to the club. It was a chilly, cool night. The moon hung high in the sky. The closer and closer she came to the club, the more she flowed with anticipation – not to mention intense arousal. She hadn't even had the time to process what had just happened with her best friend, but she knew that she loved every second of it. If Angela was okay, their friendship would still be the same and maybe even better.

The club was in a back alley of a nightclub and bar and neatly tucked away between those two buildings so that there would be no prying eyes. There was only one person stationed by the front door, one of the bouncers, Frank who made sure no vagrants would be able to enter without permission and cause any issues. Marie waved at him and said hi and he smiled at her. She came here every weekend, so they recognized her and always let her in without issues.

Marie entered the main door and into the pseudo reception area. It looked like any normal business from this side, with a receptionist stationed at the front desk. It was bright and sleek with thick wood furniture and tables. Marie said hello to the receptionist.

"The usual room, hun?" she said. She was an older woman but looked amazing for her age. She too wore a bright red lipstick.

"Yes, please. The same as last week and all the weeks before that," Marie said.

"Great, your complimentary drink and food will be stationed there in a few minutes. There's an extra little treat since you've been doing business with us for so long," the receptionist said.

"Oh, that's great! Thank you so much," Marie said. She paid the fee for the night.

"May I take your coat?" the receptionist said.

Marie handed it over to her and the receptionist put it in on a hanger in a small closet type room behind her. Many women, just like Marie, made their way over here in sexy clothes, covered up by a thick trench coat, so they installed this feature a few months before. Marie could finally breathe, it seemed. She'd been anticipating this all week and she couldn't wait to see Alex.

She walked into a hallway to the right of the receptionist. Although she was wearing such a skimpy outfit, she felt the most comfortable in this outfit and in this place. The Hot Red Club was her favorite place to be. The place in which she felt most like herself.

There were various closed doors on the left and right of the big hall before her. In the center of the room, were various couches and other types of sex furniture. There were other scantily clad women, both Marie's age and older than her. Some of them were kissing one another and others were fawning over men in their area, sitting on their laps or nibbling at their necks.

She sat down and waited for her room to be prepared before she headed inside. A few minutes later, a man came up to the door of her room pushing a big trolley. The contents of the trolley were hidden with a big white cloth draped over it. He entered the room and came out a few minutes later.

Marie took a right and entered the room marked number six. She closed the door behind her, and it was instantly silent. The good part about the Red hot club was that the private rooms one could hire were soundproof so they could make as much noise as they wanted without anyone hearing.

The room was big, decorated specifically to Marie and Alex's needs. On a small table next to the bed, various bondage implements were laid out neatly. Paddles, whips, ball gags and the like. There were two other levels to the table, and they were full of sex toys. Marie inspected a different small table on the other side of the room. Two bottles of expensive looking champagne sat in an ice bucket. Two plates covered by silver cloches were on the table too. She decided to wait for Alex to arrive before she took a peek.

Marie got comfortable and waited in participation for her master.

The door opened after what felt like an eternity of waiting and she quickly sat up straight and smiled when she saw Alex. He wore a dark suit. His raven black hair was slicked back. His facial structure was as if it were carved out of stone. He was a true god among men. He seemed slightly off today. She could feel it in the air but knew it wouldn't be appropriate to ask just yet.

"Alex, hi," Marie said. She felt a nervous lump in her throat. Although they had been seeing each other for nearly a year by now she couldn't help but feel nervous in those first few minutes together.

"Marie," he said. He sat down in front of her and loosened his tie. "I'm late. Sorry about that. Had some personal stuff to take care of. What's this?"

He looked down at the booze and food in front of them.

"It's been a year since I've been coming here so they left us a little treat," Marie said.

Alex lifted the cloche and so did Marie to reveal crepes, strawberries and a chocolate sauce beautifully presented.

"Well, isn't that sweet?" he said.

"It really is. Do you want some champagne?"

"Yes, I would like that very much, slut," he said.

Marie bit her lip and tried to hide a smile. She loved being Alex's little slut. She stood up and picked up the icy cold bottle of champagne. Applying pressure to the cork, she pushed it until it popped off. Marie bent over the table, knowing that her master would be able to see her bare ass. Her skirt was so short that it would reveal all.

She poured some champagne into the glass. Alex grabbed her ass then lightly smacked it.

"Thanks, slut. I like the outfit today. It suits you very well," Alex said.

His voice was low and gruff, it never ceased to turn her on.

"I put it on just for you. And well, because it makes me feel sexy," Marie said.

She placed the glass in front of him then hers on her side of the table. She gave Alex a smirk.

"Would you like me to do a little spin in it?"

Alex nodded.

Marie spun around in place, the momentum lifting her skirt and revealing her bare, smooth crotch.

"No panties today?" he glared at her.

"No, I was just too wet, so they started becoming very uncomfortable," she said, looking down at the floor.

He gulped all of the champagne down in one go.

"What made you so wet, Marie?" he said.

He looked her straight in the eye causing her to look away.

"Look at me," he shouted. He stood up and had his hand around her jaw, forcing her to look at him.

"Promise you won't be mad? I know you said that I have to ask permission first before I do anything with anyone, but things happened so fast and – and..."

"What the fuck did you do, slut?" he reprimanded.

He pushed her towards the bed in the center of the room, causing her to drop backwards onto it. The weight of his body suffocated her, but she loved every second of it.

"I – I fucked Angela. Well, she fucked me. I never got the chance to orgasm because I had to get ready to come see you," she whispered.

"So, you fucked someone else without asking me first?"

"Yes. I did, but I can explain – I" She was cut off.

"I don't care what your excuses are. You know the rules, Marie. Now it's time for you to get punished. Besides, I'm done with talking. We have fun first, then we talk. Those are the *rules*, stupid," he lightly slapped her face, "How many of our rules have you broken in the last twenty-four hours?"

"I'm sorry, Alex," Marie said softly.

"That's not what you call me, whore. What do you call me?"

"Master. I'm sorry, master," she whispered.

"Good. But you understand that I still have to punish you, right?"

"Yes, Master. Please punish me for being bad."

"Good girl."

Alex got off of her and flipped her around onto her stomach. He put her hands on each side of her hips, pulling her upwards so that her head was flat on the bed and her ass was up in the air. Usually, Marie would come up with silly things just so that she could receive punishment from him, she was a masochist, after all, but this time she didn't even need to make anything up to get what she wanted tonight. With her face smothered in the sheets, she smiled to herself.

"Stay," he demanded.

"Yes sir," she mumbled through the blanket.

A few moments later, he came back with a spreader bar and started restraining her with it. The cold steel nearly burned her skin as he clipped them around each of her ankles. He pulled her arms beneath her, through her legs and clipped them in. She moved her head to the side so that she could breathe. As per usual, she tugged at the restraints to ensure she couldn't get free. They were as tight as they could be, and it made her especially wet. She loved the feeling of being so helpless and weak.

Alex returned once more with a rubber paddle in his hand. He moved her skirt out of the way, pushing it down her body. He looked at the sight before him before caressing and lightly smacking and grabbing her ass. Although he was her dom, he still made sure that they played safe which was something she loved most about him.

He laced his fingers through her auburn hair, shoving her face back down into the mattress so that she couldn't expect his strikes.

The first one came, causing her to wince in pain. Then the next and the next and the next. Twenty lashes later, Alex stopped. Her ass cheeks were almost as red as her hair and they stung like hell fire. Alex kissed some of the more bruised spots on her ass before getting up and disappearing again. Marie felt herself near-dripping wet despite the pain.

Suddenly, Alex put a high powered Hitachi wand against her clit, in exactly the right spot.

"Will you come for me, whore? You want to come so bad, don't you?" Alex purred.

Upon hearing his words, she almost felt herself come instantly. He held it there until her thighs were shaking uncontrollably and she couldn't hold it in anymore. Her moans echoed throughout the room.

"Oh god. I'm gonna cum," she moaned.

"Good, don't stop yourself. Let it happen," Alex grunted.

She climaxed upon his final word, but he didn't pull the Hitachi wand away. He kept it in place. If she was getting punished, why was she allowed to even cum?

She gasped as she came again seconds later. Her wetness dripped down the wand and onto the bed.

"Keep it coming, little one," he said.

With his other hand lubed up, he massaged her asshole. At the first touch, she came yet again. When he finally felt she was ready for him to enter and he slipped a finger in, she came once more.

"Oh god, I can't take it anymore," she moaned.

She could hardly think any more. She was reduced to a true come drunk slut.

"Oh, yes you can. You are a strong whore, aren't you?"

"Yes, daddy," she whispered.

Marie lost count of the number of times she orgasmed to that little wand when Alex finally pulled it away. Marie was panting by this point and her legs couldn't stop shaking. The bruises on her ass were the furthest from her worries by now. She realized what Alex had just did: orgasm torture as a form of punishment. He'd never done that before, so it had come as a surprise. As torturous as it was, she enjoyed it and hoped they could do it again soon.

With one swift motion, Alex flipped her around onto her back. She stared deep into his eyes, practically begging him to fuck her. Slowly and meticulously, so as to punish her even more, he took his time undoing the cuffs around her wrists and ankles.

"You've made quite the mess, little one," Alex said.

"Oopsie," Marie giggled.

Alex threw the spreader bar to the side, it dropped to the floor with a loud thud. Marie wriggled with anticipation as Alex climbed on top of her. He unzipped his suit pants and pulled out his thick, long cock. Marie's breath quickened once again. She had already orgasmed so many times that she would have thought she'd be done with sex, but she realized she wanted his cock now more than ever.

She nodded at him enthusiastically to let him know that it was okay. At first, he teased her, sliding the head of his dick up and down her slick lips, tapping it against her clit. She just couldn't take it much longer, though.

"Please, please fuck me. I want you inside of me," Marie said.

"Beg harder, slut. You'll only get my cock when you beg hard enough," Alex grunted.

Marie propped herself up with her elbows and frowned at him.

"But – but I want it right now, daddy. I'm running out of patience," Marie whined.

Alex responded by continuing to rub his cock up and down her wet pussy, adding slight pressure when near her entrance, but not enough to be inside of her.

"Please," Marie moaned, "Please, there's nothing like having your cock inside of me. I just want you inside of me so badly. It's all I think about day in and day out."

He shook his head. She could see that he was trying to stifle a smile. He was enjoying the hell out of this. She'd try harder.

"I'm sorry I fucked Angela, daddy. I won't do it again without your permission. I'd never want another man's cock inside of me, though. Please remember that."

She slid her hand down her body, stopping to spread her lips for him.

"Please, please fuck me."

In an instant, with the help of her being well lubed up from cumming so many times, he shoved his cock inside of her, filling her tight hole up instantly. Marie let out a moan and spread her legs wider for the hunk inside of her. At first, he slowly pumped in and out of her, knowing that it took her a bit of time to adjust to his size. Once he found himself at a steady rhythm, he leaned forward. She wrapped her arms around his neck, one hand lacing her fingers through his hair.

While he fucked her, they kept an intense, constant gaze, never breaking eye contact. It was a kind of intimacy that Marie had never experienced with any other man in her life. As enjoyable as all the bondage was, this was one of the things that kept her coming back for more and more. He increased the pace, then moved in for a kiss. They kissed, forgetting about just about everything else in the world, until he lifted his head, and grunted. He thrust hard, hitting her cervix in the process, he came inside of her.

Again, they kissed. He slowly thrust in and out of her a few more times while their lips touched, before pulling out of her, shoving his cock back in his boxers and laying down on the bed next to her. He got comfortable, then gestured for her to come over to him. She did as he wanted, then rested her head on his chest. He kissed the top of her head, then wrapped his arms around her, squeezing her tight against him.

"How are you feeling, baby?" Alex said sincerely. His voice was softer and calmer now, as it always was after one of their sessions, as if he had become a whole different person.

"I'm okay. Feeling a little worn out, thanks to you, but I feel good," Marie said.

She listened to his heartbeat, one of the most comforting things she loved doing.

"Good. How's the ass doing? I kind of got a little carried away. You're quite bruised and might not be able to sit comfortably for a long time," he chuckled nervously.

"Honestly, I don't know if it's like a slow burn until the pain starts happening or if I'm just so satisfied and full of endorphins that I can't feel it. Besides, you know I love bruises. I love looking at them days later, knowing that you gave them to me. It turns me on so much," Marie admitted.

"Oh, I understand, yeah. It's like the mark of being owned by me."

"Exactly."

They cuddled for a while, then ate the rest of their snacks and drank the rest of the champagne. Marie admired him as he spoke about some stupid philosophical thing. She hated to admit it, but she loved Alex, so she'd let him go on rants about things, even if she didn't know much about the subject. That was something she knew proved that she loved him. She listened to him drone on about things without interrupting or losing focus.

"Anyway, enough about that. I wanted to ask, how was it with Angela? Did you enjoy it?" he asked.

"Oh! Right, yes. Actually, it was amazing. She's also very dominant, she's very similar to you. With her being a taller, bigger woman than me and all, it made it even more erotic. I loved it so much," Marie admitted.

"Hmm, getting hard just thinking about you with another woman."

"Well, she actually asked me if she could join us some time. Like, as a threesome kind of thing, but with two doms and me, the one submissive."

"Holy. Shit. That sounds incredible. Of course I'd be down, baby. You know I just get super into the moment and I'm just cruel because it's a sexual thing. I hope you remember that," Alex said. He looked at her seriously.

"Of course I understand that, love. Of course. It's just sex. I don't take those things personally, because well, frankly, it turns me on immensely."

"Okay, good. You must let me know any time I take it too far, okay?"

"Of course. There's a safe word for a reason."

"When would you like to do the double domination thing?" Alex said after a moment of thinking.

"Uh, next weekend? But if that doesn't work with you, then we can do it any other time, too. I'm happy with anything, really. You just let me know."

"Well, I was actually thinking next weekend... I'd like – I'd like to have a date," Alex said.

"A – Date?" Marie asked.

Her mouth hung open. She wasn't expecting this whatsoever.

"Yes, a date. You mentioning that we have been seeing each other for almost a year made me realize that I should have asked you this a long, long time ago," Alex said.

"Yes! Date next weekend. Double domination the weekend after," Marie shouted.

She jumped onto his lap and straddled him.

"Mm, you're excited," Alex said.

Marie bit her lip and figured out what she wanted to say.

"I wasn't sure if it would be appropriate for me to ask, since, you know, our relationship is only for Fridays and we're based on purely just sex and I was scared I'd ruin things by asking," she admitted.

"I love you though, silly," he said.

The Stranger

Yasmin was away on a business trip, in a different city, far from home, far from her husband. She took in a deep breath before stepping inside of the high-end cocktail lounge, within one of the best hotels in the city. She had a plan for the evening, and she was rather nervous about it. She decided she would have a few drinks first before she went through with it. Perhaps some liquid courage would help guide her through this potentially eventful night.

She decided on an outfit that suited the venue she was in, a couture cocktail dress, one of the best she owned. She had to bring it all the way there in a black garment bag to make sure it didn't somehow get damaged in her luggage. It was an important night, after all, so she wanted to look the part.

Although the dress was long, it was still sexy. It had a slit that made its way up her thigh, stopping just before it showed off her delicate bits. The waist had a built-in corset to show off her curves and the neckline was low, showing off her cleavage. She felt like a femme fatale in this dress, hunting her prey. At least, now, she'd use this dress to its full potential rather than it just sitting in a closet somewhere collecting dust. It cost her over five hundred dollars, after all.

Although she wasn't poor whatsoever, she still didn't like wasting money. Yasmin was one of the top lawyers in her district, defending some of the most high-risk clients in the state. Needless to say, she made a lot of money. More than what she could do with. She had everything she wanted in life and more, but she was getting older. In her late thirties now, she realized that, well, she was bored.

That was one of the problems that came along with being rich. She had everything she needed and wanted at all times. She never struggled to pull the money together to pay the bills. Or had to save up a few months to buy a good pair of shoes that would last. She never had to worry about a single thing. How could any excitement come from that? There was no struggle. There were no problems.

She felt the same with her husband, Jason. He was so good to her, too good for her, even. They were college sweethearts. They were a healthy couple. Their communication was tip top. They had a few big fights over the years, but that was normal in a good, healthy relationship. Yasmin's mother often told her once she started growing up, that couples that brag about never fighting weren't truly happy. Without fights and conflict, things couldn't be truly healthy between a couple.

After their fights, they'd talk everything through and fix their bad behaviors and such. Jason was a kind, caring man that would do anything for her. Their sex life was – she could say great, but at the same time, she felt the same about their sex life as she did about money. Jason was not a selfish lover in any way. It was just… he was too gentle and caring. Things were too good, and she was bored. Just so bored. So, she decided this weekend, she would be treating herself to someone else.

Yasmin walked up to the bar, her hips swaying and blonde curls bouncing. As she stopped in front of the young bartender, she noticed his eyes linger down to her breasts. She smirked at him and he panicked once he realized she noticed him staring.

"Sorry, just a little distracted. What can I get you, miss?" he stammered.

"Uhm, what would you suggest?" Yasmin said. She was too nervous to decide on what to have, besides, she didn't know if this place even served her favorite drink. She wasn't in the mood to look at menus at the moment, either.

She bent over the bar counter, knowing he would stare.

He made quick glances at her breasts and it made her chuckle. The attention was welcomed.

"Well, miss, what kind of experience are you looking for in your drink? Rough and hard or the opposite?"

"Hmm," – she put her finger on her chin and thought about her answer – "I'll take rough and hard."

He saw the wedding ring on her finger, his demeanor changing immediately.

"Long island iced tea will do then," he said. She could feel him judging her.

Yasmin mentally cursed herself for forgetting to take the ring off. It reminded her of her husband, and it made her feel bad for even flirting with the bartender in the first place. She let out a sigh and waited for her cocktail to be made.

"Should I open a tab for you, ma'am?"

He didn't look at her this time, his eyes slightly diverted to the side.

"Yes please. Room thirty-three. Thanks," she said.

She awkwardly walked off to a booth and sat down on the cushioned seat. She drank three Long Island Iced Teas before she finally mustered up the courage. Upon fetching the forth, she sat back down and stared at her left hand. The moment she pulled off the ring, the ball would start rolling. It was about seven in the evening, so the cocktail bar would become busier and busier. Yasmin's hands were shaking violently as she slipped the diamond ring off of her finger. She slipped the ring into a small pocket inside of her small purse, zipping it up afterwards. She closed her bag and kept it close to her.

Her hand felt so bare, so naked without the ring on it. She stared at the pale line on her finger. Her nails were perfectly manicured. Yasmin looked after herself very well, honestly, because the closer she came to turning forty, the more terrified she was of *looking old*. It was a stupid insecurity of hers that she knew she needed to work on, but at least it meant that she looked her best in every single moment. She did her hair and make-up every day. She used all the best creams and serums to keep her skin looking good.

That was something she realized as soon as she started making good money, the only reason celebrities looked so good was first of all: they had no stress to take a toll on their bodies and second of all: with enough money, they could look however they wanted. When Yasmin was younger, she thought those near thousand-dollar face creams were a gimmick, but now, she realized they truly were worth the money.

Her thoughts were interrupted when she saw a man in a suit, sitting at the same bar she was at earlier. Shortly afterwards, a near scantily clad waitress came up to her table with a tray in her hand and a drink on top of that.

"Hey, uh, that gentlemen over there said I should give this to you," the young woman said. Her hair was dark, and Yasmin could tell she had definitely been drinking on shift.

"Oh my, that one over there?" Yasmin asked, then pointed.

"Yes, exactly. The one with the dark brown hair," she said, "Do you want it?"

"Oh, yeah. Of course I would," Yasmin said.

She picked the small whiskey tumbler up and inspected it. It was her favorite: whiskey, bitters, sugar, orange juice, with ice and mashed cherries on the bottom and an orange peel wedged into the edge of the glass. There was even an extra maraschino cherry atop the ice, stem attached. Once the waitress went back to the bar, she said a few words to the man. The waitress smiled and nodded her head at him before she receded into the back of the cocktail lounge, out of sight.

The man then spun around in his seat, the same cocktail as hers in his hand. He leaned his back against the bar, before raising his glass in her direction. Yasmin returned the gesture. It made her feel all warm and squishy inside. No man had ever done that for her before, Yasmin thought that random men flirting in the form of buying drinks was only reserved for the movies. Regardless, it sure made her feel special. He was around about her age, maybe a few years younger.

His hair was brown and neatly combed into a slick side part. He wore a gray suit perfectly tailored to his well-cared for body. His face was shaven, barring the five o'clock shadow peeking through.

His features were strong and well chiseled. His smile was charming.

Needless to say, he was an attractive man and she wanted him. Thoughts of Yasmin's husband were in the far reaches of her mind. This handsome stranger was all she wanted, and she wanted him now. The heat between her legs was steadily growing, almost too much for her to handle any longer.

She called him over with a come-hither motion. He stood up, slicked a stray hair back into place and walked over to her with one hand in his pocket. She bit her lip when he came close enough for her to smell his cologne. It was musky and reeked of masculinity.

"Well, hello there, beautiful," was the first thing he said.

Yasmin hesitated, unsure of how to reply. Her cheeks glowed red and hot. She wasn't used to this and she didn't know what to do. She hadn't quite prepared for this.

"Hmm, not much of a talker, are ya?" he asked.

He sat down next to her, both their backs to the wall of the rest of the cocktail bar. They were semi-secluded where they were seated, with dividers between them and the other booth seats.

"Thank you for the drink," she said softly, "What made you choose an old fashioned?" Her voice was shaky and unsure.

"Of course, I could tell that a woman like you would enjoy a classy drink like that," he took a sip of his own drink while making eye contact with her, "I hope you like it."

"Oh, of course. It's absolutely delicious. Thank you."

"Besides, I couldn't stand to let you sit here all by yourself any longer. What's an alluring woman like you sitting alone in a place like this?"

"I could ask you the same thing," she teased, "I'm here for a week on business. They flew me over on Friday so I could be settled before I get thrown into a barrage of meetings and such."

"Hmm, so a career woman, then? That's sexy. What do you do?" he asked. He spoke in a low and gruff full-throated manner. He was sure and serious about every single word that came out of his mouth. His blue eyes were cold and filled with primal desire for the woman before him. This stranger was turning out to be exactly her type, strong, manly and most of all, mysterious.

"I'm a lawyer, allegedly," Yasmin joked.

The man laughed, "And a sense of humor? Damn."

"What do you do?"

"Oh, not as cool as a lawyer, I'm an accountant. But, I'm good at more than just numbers," he said, looking deep into her eyes.

He put his hand on her thigh, the one exposed by the slit in her dress. His hands were warm and rough. Yasmin bit her lip, she wasn't quite sure how to react to his advances, though, so she took another sip of her drink. Next, she fished out the stemmed maraschino cherry, putting it between her lips and sucking on it while making eye contact with the stranger. She batted her long, curled eyelashes at him. His hand slowly crept up her thigh. He stopped just before he reached her crotch. Hopefully inconspicuously, she slightly spread her legs.

"Are you staying at this hotel, too? Or are you just at this lounge for the hell of it?" he spoke, as he came closer and closer to her sopping wet cunt. His gaze never faltered from hers.

"Yeah, I'm in room thirty-three, actually," she said. Her breath quickened, his fingers softly traced over her outer labia, teasing her desperate bits.

"Oh, is that so? I'm on the same floor, close to your room. Maybe I could pay you a visit some time."

"Oh, yes," she moaned softly as he found her wet hole, slipping inside of her without hesitation, "Yes, I would like that very much."

Slowly, he slid his finger in and out of her, so as to not arouse suspicion to what they were doing. Fortunately, the bar was quite busy, so no one would pay them any attention. The sheer thought of doing something so scandalous in front of so many people excited her. He brought his face close to her ear and whispered.

"I'll warn you, though, I like to be rough. If you slipped me your room key, I'd come into your room and take you no matter what you are busy with, be it on a business call or you in the bath. I like to take what I want when I want it. And I want you."

He nibbled on her earlobe before pulling away. Yasmin's breath was taken away: all the words she would have liked to say in this moment, all the words she fantasized about saying were caught in the back of her throat.

"I don't know what to say," she said softly.

"Don't say anything, slut. Just enjoy it while you can," he said.

His harsh words sent hot flushes all throughout her body. As she bit her lip again, he slipped a second finger inside of her, stretching her out. She fantasized about his big cock inside of her, filling her up to the brim.

She downed her drink, he did too.

"Should we head up to my room?" she asked.

"Of course we should," he whispered, "I want to fuck you so hard. I love that you're not even wearing panties. You were hunting for your prey tonight weren't you, you filthy whore?"

"Yes, I was expecting to get laid. I mean, look at this dress. Look at me. Can't you see I'm practically begging for someone to bend me over and have their way with me?"

"Well, I'm one lucky man," he said.

Yasmin grabbed his hand and led him to the elevator. There was a moment of silence before the elevator door closed. In seconds, the stranger pinned her against the mirrored wall of the elevator, kissing all up her neck and breasts. He pushed his crotch up against hers, turning her on even more. She hadn't even touched him, yet he was hard for her. It made her feel sexy and desirable. She couldn't wait to see what was hidden in those expensive suit pants.

The elevator doors slid open with a loud *ding* and they separated from one another when they saw a family standing in front of them. Embarrassed, she grabbed his hand and pushed past them, leading him to her hotel room.

She inserted the card to her room, then let him in. He walked a few steps before turning to face her. Yasmin had her back to the hotel door. She looked at him seductively. She sauntered over to him. Her arms wrapped around her waist, before he placed his hands on her ass and squeezed. He lifted her up and she wrapped her legs around him as he picked her up and carried her over to the bed. She kissed the nape of his neck, occasionally sucking hard on his skin, leaving small bruises in his flesh. She softly chuckled. That'll be an embarrassing thing for him to deal with in the morning.

He turned around and dropped her onto the bed. She landed with a few bounces. He stood up and inspected the marvel before him.

He loosened his tie then pulled it off of his neck.

"Get higher on the bed. I'm going to tie you up," he said sternly.

She did as she was told and scooted upwards. The stranger looped the tie around the bed frame, before wrapping it around her wrists, crossing in between each one to be sure it was secure. He tugged at the makeshift cuffs.

"Nice and snug," he said.

"What are you going to do to me?" she said, concerned.

"Have my every which way with you, my dear," he whispered.

Yasmin bit her lip again, causing it to sting. She had bitten her lip so many times that night that it was going raw.

Slowly and carefully, he unbuckled then slipped off each of her high heels. He caressed her smooth legs, moving up between her thighs. From inside of his suit, he pulled out a small pocket knife. Yasmin blinked rapidly at the blade as he withdrew the blade, the shiny metal glistening in the bright white hotel lights.

"W-what are you going to do with that?" she inquired.

"Whatever I want to," he said. He shook his head. "Do you have any scarves? I'm tired of hearing your complaints."

"I – I'm sorry, I'll stop. I'm just nervous."

"Shut the fuck up. Where are the scarves? Preferably longer ones," he spat.

"There," she looked in the direction of where she would have pointed, if her hands weren't tied. Her heart was beating heavier in her chest by now, not out of arousal, but fear.

He rummaged through the nearby drawer before finding a red scarf. He mumbled a 'This'll do.' before coming back to her. He forced her mouth open by applying pressure on each side of her jaw, before placing the material in her open mouth, then tying it around the back of her head. Yasmin bit down on the soft silk scarf. He got on top of her again and stared at the bound-up goddess before him.

The blade tickled up her thigh, stopping at the seam of the slit of her dress. She lifted her head to see what he was doing. She shook her head violently, making a few muffled sounds but nothing worthwhile came through the saliva-soaked gag.

The stranger held the fabric taut, blade side up. Yasmin tensed up as the first bit of fabric started ripping. She tried pleading with the stranger to stop but the gag prevented her from saying any words. She felt helpless, hopeless, and weak.

The blade slowly ran diagonally up her chest. Her dress had been split in two. He held the knife in his hand and pulled the fabric to the side to reveal her bra. He smiled at her and made direct eye contact with her while he cut the bra off of her. She felt a relief at the loss of pressure on her breasts.

"Hmm, your tits are incredible," he moaned.

His rough hands touched her breasts, grabbing them hard. Despite the pain, Yasmin enjoyed the way he treated her. Despite the fear and anxiety, deep down, she enjoyed this. She had never had sex with anyone else but her husband. When they started dating in college, she had lost her virginity to him. Still, he was so soft and gentle with her.

The stranger, on the other hand, didn't care. He was going to take what he wanted, and he didn't care if she had anything to say about it. She could feel the wetness between her thighs, each time she moved them or rubbed them together they were slick and smooth.

The stranger didn't kiss her breasts like her husband usually would, instead, he left red bite marks behind that would likely form bruises. Yasmin decided to play along with this fantasy and tugged at the tight restraints, writhing in place as he steadily made his way between her legs.

Slowly but surely, he unbuckled his belt and took his pants off. This man was in no rush. He knew that she couldn't fight it so why would he hurry?

Yasmin looked on in awe of the sheer size of his cock. She could practically see the veins in his cock throbbing. He was enjoying this, a lot.

"Spread your legs," he demanded.

Yasmin refused. In response, she clamped her legs shut.

"I said spread your goddamned legs!" he shouted.

Yasmin whimpered, finally complying. Slowly she spread her legs apart. He lifted her knees. He stared at her sopping wet cunt, slowly stroking his big cock.

With his other hand, he rubbed her clit. She wriggled underneath the pressure of his fingers, but it just added to the pleasure. Somehow knowing that she was close to orgasm, he suddenly stopped to shove his cock inside of her. He pushed her legs back over her head and fucked her harder than she's ever been fucked before.

His cock slid in and out of her slick cunt with ease. His cock hit her G-spot with the angle he was fucking her. Her moans were muffled by the gag in her mouth. By now the scarf was soaked with her spit. She bit down on it hard as he rubbed her clit with his thumb.

Yasmin buckled under him, her back arching and her legs shaking as she reached orgasm. He grunted when her muscles tensed and relaxed around his cock. He pulled out of her, then shoved two fingers inside of her, furiously thrusting his fingers up against her G-spot. Yasmin's eyes rolled to the back of her head as all the tension within her released, to her surprise, she squirted. The clear, warm liquid sprayed onto the bed.

Gently, he pulled his fingers out of her. With one hand he yanked the gag from her mouth. His hand firmly took her by the chin, his thumb tracing the outline of her plump lips. He pulled down and shoved her mouth open, then his fingers that were inside of her plunged into her mouth. She lapped up her wetness off of him. She was hungry for it, lapping it up as if it were sweet honey.

"Good slut," the stranger said.

She moaned around his fingers.

"Absolutely exquisite," he groaned, "But I'm not done with you yet."

His strong hands gripped her thighs firmly, rotating her around so that she was on her knees and her ass was facing him. The tie around her wrists tightened as she flipped around, causing even more strain. Her arms were lifted above her head, her face forced into the mattress. With her knees together and her ass high up in the air, it formed a perfect heart shape. The stranger admired her figure.

As if thinking she were too perfect and wanting to taint her all too perfect physique, he picked up his belt and struck her suddenly. She inhaled sharply. It wasn't what she expected to happen, which made it hurt even more. Immediately, red began forming on the pale flesh of her plump ass. Again, he struck harder this time, testing the limits. She moaned, not out of pain, but pleasure. She'd never been handled this way – never been so man handled and treated so badly. It was thrilling and exciting for her to be treated like such a slut. She bit her lip, preparing for the next impact. This time, when she bit her lip, she drew blood. Her mouth tasted of copper. As she was distracted by that thought, he struck again, giving her two lashings on the opposite cheek. These stung harder than before and she inhaled sharply through her clenched teeth.

He ran a finger from her clit all the way up her slit.

"You're still so wet," he chuckled, "You're really enjoying this, aren't you?"

"Yes, sir," she whispered, "You felt so good inside of me. You're so big and I love how full you made me feel."

He grunted in response. He seemed to have really liked the way she responded to that.

"Good girl," he said.

She felt some movement on the bed.

She gasped as suddenly the tip of his cock breached her lips. He shoved his cock inside of her wet cunt and fucked her ferociously. He was done playing around with his toy – he was ready to have his own release. He fucked her in a primal, deviant manner. He gripped her hips tightly, guiding himself in and out of her.

He fucked her so well that she was succumbed to a groaning mess.

She could tell that he was nearing his own climax by the loud groans escaping the back of his throat.

"Oh, yes, fuck me harder," she moaned, "Come inside of me."

He increased the pace for the last few moments before his cock twitched inside of her and he came.

His breaths were just as heavy as hers. He collapsed next to her on the bed.

Yasmin went to the bathroom to clean herself up. She grabbed a comfortable shirt from her suitcase, then lay next to him. He put his arm out, gesturing for her to lay in his arms. She rested her head on his shoulder and looked up at his deep blue eyes. His face was plastered with a big smile.

"That was amazing, honey," she said.

"No, you were amazing," he said softly.

"I liked the extra touch of cutting my dress off. You'll have to buy me a new one, though. It was my fanciest dress," she giggled.

"Pfft. I already planned for that. I had it all planned out, Yasmin. Did you have a good time, though? I hope I didn't go too far."

"I loved every second of it, Jason. I was kind of hesitant to try this when you mentioned it first, but it ended up being everything I wanted and more. I like you being rough. I would love to do this again sometime," Yasmin said.

"Well, you mentioned that you wanted to try something different. I loved being someone else, you know? It was as if it were easier for me to be rough since it wasn't really *me,* if that makes sense. I always worry about hurting you or being too rough, but it just came so easily today," Jason, her husband said.

"Thank you for going out of your comfort zone just for me, honey," Yasmin said.

They had planned this for months and decided that her being away on a business trip was the perfect time for it. As she had told him, their little affair fantasy role play was everything she wanted and more. They had grown closer because of it.

Mason's Plaything

Mason was a twenty-seven-year-old man. Within the modern age of dating, he found himself struggling to find someone to settle down with. He was a six-foot three man, who looked after his body, had a lot of friends, a booming career and he even made time for hobbies. This and more, brought him a lot of dates.

The only problem was that only about two out of fifty women he's tried to be with ever went through with a second date. Those two, never went through with a third date. He was lonely and lacked true human connection. As things were in the modern times, sex would definitely happen on the first date. That was a given. After having sex with him, the women never came back. Those two women who had a second date with him, had decided to save themselves for the second date. They also never came back. They would enjoy his company at dinner, his jokes, his life stories. All would be well at first.

He wasn't unattractive. He was strong, he was charming, he had a sense of humor. He had green eyes and pitch-black hair. As some people would tell him, he had the whole *dark and mysterious* vibe about him. Women liked that. That's why he could land himself so many dates.

It hurt him to the core that he couldn't keep a romantic relationship with a woman going. He was getting older now, with each year that went by leaving him with a sense of doom at the thought of having to spend the rest of his life alone. The longer he waited, he felt, the less chance he had at finding the perfect woman to marry.

Although he was *nontraditional* in the bedroom, he still wanted to marry a wonderful woman he loved and spend the rest of his life with her. He scrolled through Tinder, swiping left and right, hoping to find someone who would maybe, just maybe stick around. A woman he'd been chatting to for a while, Sabrina, sent a message through. They'd been talking to one another for weeks over text but hadn't met yet. He didn't even know what her voice sounded like.

Most of his previous dates would instantly want to meet up on the next available date he had free, so this could have been a sign that she could be the one. Perhaps, they could have a third, fourth, fifth date.

Sabrina was taking things slowly.

That could have possibly been a good thing. He was growing to like her, or at least the words she put on the screen. She seemed like an interesting person, having just completed her law degree and starting her life as a lawyer. She was witty and intelligent. Strong.

Interesting.

That was too, what the other women he had tried dating had lacked. Sure, they were attractive, dare he say, out of his league, but they only cared about getting in his pants so they could subsequently get their grubby little paws on his money. He could see it from the look in their eyes the moment they set foot in his penthouse apartment – they wanted to run him dry if they could.

But then things would go wrong after they fucked, and he'd never see them again.

He texted her. They had a conversation about how work was going and how life was treating her. Since she had an actual career, she was quite busy, so she would sometimes go weeks without speaking to him. In a way, that could have been what made him so fond of her and him wanting so desperately for it to work out. The longer he waited, the more he thought about her and the more he fantasized about how good things could be.

After a few fun conversations about stupid clients and silly mishaps, she finally brought it up. She asked him if he wanted to meet up with her. He replied instantly, almost so fast that it could have seemed desperate. He couldn't wait.

"Alright, babe. This weekend, then. I will book everything and plan it all. We'll make a day of it on Saturday. How does that sound?" he asked.

"Sure, that sounds great! I would love to. I suppose having a whole day to spend together is great for a first meeting. We can *truly* get to know each other! What should I wear?" she said.

"Wear anything that makes you feel good! I'm not fussy. Comfortable. Sexy. Cute. Whatever your heart desires, sweetheart."

"Hmm. I'll think about it."

She was the same age as him and seemed quite mature too. Something in the back of his mind bugged him, though. Why was she also single, at the age of twenty-seven? Perhaps he was just being too pessimistic. Someone being single didn't necessarily need to mean that there was something wrong with them.

Just because he was single because there was something wrong with him – he stopped himself from thinking about it further. He would be good on the weekend. He would behave. He wouldn't scare her off. Mason promised that to himself. How hard could it really be just to control himself? He waited in anticipation for Saturday.

***

Mason, among many other facets of his being, was a hopeless romantic. He made sure to look good and dress well for his dates. He brought flowers every time. He made sure to smell good. Mason opened doors, pulled out chairs, complimented them. He would take his women out to the best places he could afford, which was *a lot*. Mason was the owner of a startup company that grew in popularity like hellfire over just a mere three years since its start. He was a millionaire. He could have lived in a mansion, but that life wasn't really for him. He liked living in a penthouse; he loved the view overlooking the city, especially at night. Mason loved that the entire section of wall that faced the city was purely made of windows. It stretched from his living room, all the way to the kitchen, to his bedroom. In every room of his house, except for his bedroom, he had a view. There was nothing quite like waking up to a glorious view like that.

It was Saturday and he woke up early to prepare for his date with Sabrina. He purchased flowers, made sure his apartment was spick and span in case she wanted to come home with him, and got ready for the date. He decided on a white shirt, with the sleeves rolled up, and a dark pair of pants. He patted on some cologne. Everything seemed so perfect so far. Their date would go well. Everything was going to be fine. He checked himself out in the mirror, took a deep breath, and left the apartment with the flowers in hand.

He got inside his 1969 Pontiac Firebird. Old school and expensive, but he loved it. He'd looked after it so well, that it even still had the all too familiar new car smell. There was nothing more attractive than some of the old school cars. Newer models were just so – uninspired in comparison.

Sabrina would be ready soon, so he drove to her apartment. She was just a little way out of town. As soon as he drove into her stomping ground, he was filled with a strange pit in his chest. She lived in a shit hole town. Every person he drove past seemingly stared him down until he was out of site, as if they were plotting how to steal it from him.

He pushed the uncomfortable feeling aside. He had a girl to romance. So, what if she lived in a bad part of town? She was soon to be a successful lawyer. Everyone had to start at a place like this as some point in time. He understood how tough it was to get a job straight out of college. He assured himself that everything was fine. Everything was going to be just okay.

He parked outside of the building that he had been guided to. It was tall and dilapidated. It didn't stand tall and proud like his did, it was slouched and sad.

He locked the door behind him before making his way inside the creaky front gate. She was on the fifth floor. There was no elevator, he had to climb the stairs there. Babies cried and old men coughed. Strange smells emitted from some apartments, he didn't even dare figure out what they could be.

He knocked on her door. She opened a minute later, wearing a nice, sleek dress that hugged her petite body. It was red and left nothing to the imagination. Her breasts were much bigger than he had imagined from her pictures. Her hair was soft and shiny, a silky, healthy light brown. Definitely a calm comfort against all he had to endure to come here.

"Hey," she said sweetly. Her voice was higher pitched and more feminine than he had imagined.

"Hi, Sabrina. I brought you flowers!" he said.

He handed them to her. She smiled in return, taking the large bouquet in her arms.

"Aww, these are beautiful. I'll put them in a vase, then we can head out. Is that alright?" she asked.

"Of course," he said.

"Come in then, come in," she said excitedly.

He stepped inside. Her apartment wasn't as bad as he had imagined it being considering what he had walked past on his way into it. He bit his tongue. He couldn't mention how much of a shit hole her town was. That would just be rude. Besides, he was just coming from a place of privilege. He had money. That's what money gave him. Comfort and security.

If this was all that she could afford, it was fine. It didn't mean she was any less of a person than he was. His pre-date nerves were just setting in and he was overthinking things again.

"You're a lot more handsome than your pictures make you look," she said. She stood at her sink with her back to him. He could tell from the way that she said it, that she was smiling while she spoke.

"Thank you. And you're more gorgeous than I could have ever imagined," he said.

She placed the vase on the small dining table in her living room. Sabrina grabbed her purse, then fixed her hair in the mirror that was in the hallway, near the door.

"Right then, should we get going?" she said.

He nodded at her. She looped her arm in his as they walked down the five floors and towards the car. He wondered if it was a safety thing considering all the ruffians in the area, or a thing of just being physically affectionate.

They got in the car. He wasn't usually this awkward and silent. Things were already off to a bad start and he felt like a total dickhead for it. He drove her to one of his favorite places in the city. He knew she would love it.

"Right. You're quiet. It's because of where I live, right?" she said abruptly.

He inhaled sharply. He wasn't expecting her to be so upfront, but he kind of loved it. He loved a woman that would speak her mind, no matter how awkward things became as a result.

"Oh man, I feel like such a dick. I'm sorry. I just, I don't know if this makes sense or if you've ever experienced it before, but when I step foot inside of certain places, and it feels *off* it makes me feel kind of weird," he admitted.

"You mean, like that weird heaviness in your chest? Like, someone's got a heavy grip on your heart? Something like that?" she asked.

"Yes. Yes, exactly. So, you know what I mean, then? It's nothing against you, it's just, I felt that when I stepped foot inside your apartment block. Actually, this town."

"Nah, man. I get it. I feel the same things sometimes. They're called the Murder Flats for a reason," she chuckled.

"The what!?"

"The Murder Flats. People have been killed there," she said.

"Wow. Why do you stay there then?" he asked, genuinely curious.

"Honestly, my grandpa used to own it, and passed it down to me when he passed away. I'm kind of using it as a way to save extra cash before I move into an actual house. It's difficult to think about buying a house when you are busy paying rent, you know?"

"Yeah, I get that. But are you safe? I understand the need to save and all, but it really is a little rough around there," he asked.

"Well, it used to be a really nice area when my grandpa bought the apartment. Just went to shit over the years. Everyone in the area knows him – they won't mess with me. He was one of those cool, scary old men, ya know? Besides, I have training in defending myself if anything happens," she said.

"Oh, okay, that's pretty good. I'm happy about that. Quite an interesting grandpa. Wish mine was as interesting. I just remember that he was cruel," he paused for a moment, "And he smoked a lot. Still remember that smell."

"Oof. Yeah, chain smokers. Not good. Anyway, sorry about getting so heavy on ya there, honey. I just wanted to clear things up a little, so you didn't think I was crazy."

"No, Sabrina. I didn't think you were crazy. You seem great and I like you a lot so far," he admitted.

Mason found that over the years, the best talks he'd have with people were on long drives in his car. So, he would often take the long route, sometimes circling around the block a few times if he realized they needed more time to talk. The passengers wouldn't even notice since they were both just having such a good conversation.

He had done that just now, with Sabrina. Already, he counted too many things that he loved about her. Her honesty. The way she sat in the leather seat of his car. How she nervously twirled her brown locks when speaking about something uncomfortable.

Maybe he was just falling for her too hard, too quick.

They arrived at their destination. He opened the door for her, like a gentleman, and helped her out. He couldn't help but stare as her tight dress rode up her thighs as she swung her legs out. He noted that her panties were bright while. He was already pulling a semi-hard on in his pants.

He'd rip those off of her and shove them in her mouth later so she couldn't scream.

He shook his head, as if to physically shake the deviant thoughts in his head away.

Not now. Not today. Please, he begged himself, *just be normal, Mason. Be normal.*

"Hmm, such a gentleman, huh?" she chimed.

"Anything for a beautiful woman like you, Sabrina," he said. He did a jokey bow for her and it made her giggle.

"You're too kind," she said.

"No, I am not. Women deserve to be treated nicely at times," he said. He meant what he said. He was conflicted between his deviant, lustful side, and the hopeless romantic side that wanted to give a girl what she deserved, respect and love.

"Well, aren't you the charming one?"

He gave his key to a valet to park his car inside the building. The valet was a short, chubby man but seemed like he could be trusted. Mason instinctively slipped him a twenty dollar note for his trouble.

She looped her arm in his as he led her up the stairs. They walked a few flights up the side of the building until they reached the roof. He held her hand and helped her up the last step. Her face lit up once she saw where he had taken her. A high-end restaurant and bar on the top of a tall building, with a view of the city from where they would eat. The bar was separated off to the left of the seating area, and people would have to fetch their own drinks.

There was a cocktail bar as well as having an open plan kitchen, something he loved. It was great being able to watch the magic happen in the kitchen, trying to guess if they were busy with your meal or someone else's. A greeter told them a waiter would be with them shortly and that they could be seated where he had reserved a spot. The restaurant was awfully busy at the time, but that was good. Mason loved the hustle and bustle and the background noise that came along with it.

He had been in empty restaurants before and they were kind of eerie. When going out to eat, that all too familiar sound was expected.

"Woah, this is lovely," she said as he pulled the chair out for her to sit down.

As he pushed her chair in, he noticed that she was light and small. So easy and fun for him to have his way with her however he pleased.

She seemed happy and not nervous whatsoever. He liked that too. A woman with confidence. A woman who held her head high.

He let her have the seat that overlooked the view. He wanted to be able to see the twinkle in her eye as she watched on at the night.

"This is amazing, Mason. Thank you for bringing me here," she said sincerely, "What do they serve here?"

"Japanese food. I hope that's to your taste – I usually take girls out to a simpler place for the first date until I know what they like. I know that you like Japanese food, though, so I settled on this in the end," Mason said.

"Hmm. Take a lot of girls on dates, do you?" she raised an eyebrow at him.

"No! Not really. Shit, I didn't mean for it to come out like that. I'm not some douche bag," Mason scratched the back of his head nervously. He was really losing his skill in charming women. Doing the same thing over and over again was getting to him. Doing the same thing over and over expecting different results was one of the definitions of insanity, after all.

"I'm teasing you, stupid. You're a grown man. I don't care if you go on dates every weekend. What happened in the past doesn't matter, it's what happens between us that truly means something. Honestly, I can't stand those kinds of people that demand to know every tiny detail of my life. Often, it's brought up in later arguments and it just makes things messy, you know?" she said.

How insightful.

"Yeah, you're right. Besides, the person you are a year ago isn't the same person you are now. Not to mention, when in a relationship, you become a whole other person entirely compared to when you're single. So why judge someone for who they were when they were single? If you're with them, it shouldn't matter."

"Exactly. Gosh, what do you think about ordering some drinks? I've actually had such a tough week and need some down time. I'll pay for the cab, so you don't have to drive drunk," Sabrina said.

"You don't need to worry about that, Sabrina. I'll sort it out. And of course, I'd love to have a few drinks. What's your drink of choice? I'll order it at the cocktail bar," he said.

"Bit strange having a cocktail bar inside of a Japanese restaurant. Anyway, uh, something sweet. Strawberry daiquiri? Or something like that, anyway," she said.

"I thought the same thing when I came here the first time. They try to stay true to tradition in their food though, at least. They still need to cater to the alcoholics, though," Mason said, "If the waiter comes, I'll have some golden parcels for a starter. Order yourself anything. Dinner's on me."

He walked off to the bar. A few people were seated on some bar stools, other at some tall circular tables, here just to get sloshed. He pushed through the crowd and stopped in front of the bar. The bartender was busy serving someone else, so he took a seat on the only available stool, next to a curvy, tall woman. He waited patiently, occasionally sneaking glances at the woman next to him. He couldn't help it. There was something that drew him to her.

Perhaps it was the overly feminine aura she emitted. Or the way she sat so up straight, a posture usually only seen in ballerinas. She was older though, perhaps in her mid-thirties to early forties, apparent from the smile lines on her face. It was beautiful, though. It showed that she had lived a good life and smiled a lot. A red lip accompanied it, along with a neatly pinned up, curled hair do.

She was alluring. Dare he say, a delectable MILF.

She looked over at him, but he didn't look away.

"What are ya looking at, handsome? Do ya need somethin'?" she asked. Many of her words had a distinct southern twinge to them.

"I need to rip your clothes off and fuck you till you can't think about anything but me," he said in his head.

He couldn't say that to a stranger, so he lied instead. "Oh, just looking. What are you doing here, sitting all alone?"

"I'm just getting pissed because I don't want to go home alone. At least I'm around some people now," she said honestly.

"Hmm, that's unfortunate, a woman like you doesn't deserve to be alone on a Saturday evening," Mason said.

"What's a woman like me?"

He eyed her up and down. Her cinched in waist, her abundant breasts. Her big smile, framed by deep red lips. Her near white-blonde hair.

"You're a seductress," he said.

The bartender made his way over to where Mason was, wiping his hands on a white cloth.

"What can I get you, sir?" he asked.

"Top shelf whiskey and a strong strawberry daiquiri, please," Mason said.

"You're on a date," the Seductress said, "Aren't you?"

Mason sighed. He was. He was on a date with a wonderful, smart woman, but he was flirting with a MILF. It was a cold, wake up call that he needed to get his shit together.

"Uh, yeah. I am," Mason admitted.

"First date, isn't it?" she smiled at him.

"How do you know that?"

"You're wearing your best shirt and your best cologne that you save for special occasions," she chuckled.

"Well, miss, you're a perceptive one," he said. His cock throbbed and he hoped it would go away soon.

"I'm known for it."

The drinks he ordered were set in front of him and he made his way back to Sabrina without saying goodbye to the MILF. Mostly out of embarrassment for flirting with her while he was on a date, secondly, because if he didn't leave, he'd take her home instead. He just *knew* she wore a matching set of lacy lingerie beneath her clothing, a garter belt to match. He knew from just seeing a little bit of the lace lining of the top of her thigh high stockings.

Sabrina smiled as she sat back down. She paled in comparison to the utter goddess he had seen at the bar. He forced himself to forget about her. She was a great person. He needed to stop being such a horny bastard.

"What took you so long, Mason? Everything okay?" Sabrina asked.

"Ah, sorry to keep you waiting. Long line at the bar. I got what you wanted, though!" he handed her drink to her. His hand hurt from touching the cold, icy glass for so long. He rubbed his hands together to get feeling back into it again.

"No worries," she said. She tucked an artificial curl behind her ear. "I ordered starters, by the way."

"Oh, great! I wanted to ask, what made your week so tough? Want to talk about it?"

"Ugh," she sighed, "You know those difficult people that won't work with you no matter how hard you try, constantly making unrealistic demands and getting mad when they can't be met?"

"Oh, yes. I know them all too well. Mostly men or women in their fifties or sixties. Miserable bastards," he said. It was true, he dealt with those people in his company at least twice a month. Entitled people that thought just because they were older, they could do and ask for whatever they wanted without consequence.

"Well, since I'm a newbie in the lawyer world, trying to make my way up, my boss is throwing all the evil clients my way, the ones that no one else wants to work with. This asshole is treating me like shit because legally, I cannot help him sue his neighbor for building a shed on his own property. Said neighbor had gotten all the permits for building beforehand. But mister Asshole doesn't want to stand for that," Sabrina said.

"What a moron. What are you going to do with him?" Mason asked.

"Dude, he basically stalks me, I swear. He just keeps coming back to me with new things, hoping some tiny detail will help him sue his sweet neighbor. I spoke to the neighbor and everything, and he's just a sweet old man that doesn't want any trouble. God, I hate this guy. He's called me so many derogatory things but there's nothing I can do about it because well, it's my job. My boss is just as much of a moron as him. But he's been in the industry for ten plus years, so his word is law," Sabrina said.

"Man, that's the reason I'm my own boss. I just couldn't bow down to someone else, I swear. If anyone treated me like shit just because they were my boss and an authority, I'd punch them in the face. I'd never last in that environment," Mason admitted.

"I get that, honestly, if I weren't so patient, I'd do the same. But it is what it is, you know? These are the first steps before eventually, I can start my own practice. It's all just progress. Going through the motions in life. Sometimes, you have to do shit you don't want to do just because you *have to.*"

"Yeah, makes sense. That is true."

Her dirty mouth was charming. He wondered what kind of verbiage she used in bed.

But would she even go home with him tonight? He couldn't expect it just because they were on a date. It wouldn't be fair to expect that of her.

But, God, was he hankering for some good pussy. He hadn't fucked anyone but his own hand in weeks. He needed that closeness. That intimacy. As good as masturbating was, it paled in comparison to actually being with a woman. He stared at The Seductress that still sat at the bar counter, drinking gin. Her posture stayed straight. She spoke to a young man, shortly leaving with him after. Deep down, it made Mason kind of sad. He'd never see her again. What an intriguing woman.

He reminded himself to focus on things right in front of him.

"Focus, Mason. Keep your fucking dick in your pants and enjoy her company," he demanded from himself. He chose to forget about the blonde-haired goddess from then on and focus on the woman in front of him.

They got to know each other better throughout dinner. The drinks flowed near endlessly as they forgot about all their responsibilities and troubles. He genuinely enjoyed her company. She was a lot more entertaining in person than over text. Her sense of humor shined through. While she spoke of something she was passionate about, he almost felt like he was falling for her.

Her eyes lit up when she spoke of her family that lived back in Brazil, although he could see the sadness of being apart from them mixed throughout.

She was a good, hard working person. She didn't know about his money or what he specifically did for a living and he wanted to keep it that way at least for a while. If money weren't in the mix, maybe she'd like him for who he was, instead of his fortune.

Would that be lying? He wondered. Lying by omission was a thing. Did he want their potential relationship to be based on lies? He was five and a half whiskeys down. He could already feel himself nearing the point of loss of inhibitions.

"Sabrina, I hope you enjoyed the food," Mason said. Although he was drunk, he didn't look it.

She patted at the corner of her mouth with a cloth napkin, hoping not to mess up her lipstick.

"Of course. This place is incredible, Mason. Thank you for introducing me to this. I don't really get out that much anymore. It's just work, work, work and no play."

Her brown eyes stared up at him. She gave him *that* look. She wanted him to fuck her. She kept shifting in her seat, as if her panties were so wet that she was uncomfortable. She bit her lip occasionally, played with her hair as they stared each other in the eyes.

She was ready.

"Pardon if this is too forward, but would you like to head back to my place for a few more drinks to end the night off?" Mason said. Even though he knew she would say yes with no hesitation, he would be a gentleman about it.

"I'm so happy you finally asked," she purred, "I would love that, Mason. Besides, you've seen *my* apartment. I would love to see yours."

"Hmm, sounds like a fair deal, sweetheart. I'll settle the bill and we can go on our merry way," Mason said.

She nodded quickly. She couldn't fucking wait to get in his pants, could she? What a filthy slut, throwing herself at a man she had just met today. He paid up, leaving their waiter a nice, fat tip. He hurried, impatient to get home and have his way with her.

With alcohol in his system, he could no longer suppress the deviant thoughts in his head. As they taxied to his apartment building, he reminded himself that even if he had those thoughts, he could still control those actions. It was easy. He could do this.

The taxi's brakes came to a screeching stop in front of the big building. It was tall, lit up by the people that lived inside. She craned her neck to look at the top of the building.

"Holy shit," she breathed, "You actually live here?"

"Yup. Follow me, Brina," he said.

"Sure. I'd get lost in there if I didn't. How many floors are there in it anyway?" she asked.

"Thirteen," he said as they stepped inside of the cozy elevator.

"Woah. Okay," she said. She leaned on his shoulder. From the corner of his eye, he could see her staring up at him admirably. Her entire world had changed, knowing that he lived in a place like this. Only the best of the best lived here. Millionaires, billionaires and celebrities. He could tell she was wondering how much money he actually made and how he made it.

"You're on the thirteenth floor?" she asked.

"Yes, I am," he said. He wasn't paying attention to the conversation. He was just thinking about fucking her. Thinking about what she was wearing underneath that tight, red dress. She stood on her tip toes and brought his face down to hers. For a moment, she just stared.

She pushed her body against his. Her crotch brushed up against his hard on and when she felt it, she pushed up against him even harder, knocking him against the back of the elevator. She ran her fingers through his hair, lust apparent in her eyes.

She kissed him. It was sloppy, but good. Her tongue brushed against his and he welcomed it. Mason grabbed at her ass, accidentally pulling her dress up in the process. He didn't hesitate to rub her over her panties. He found her clit, applying pressure and rubbing up against it. She'd pull away to take in a breath or to stop herself from moaning in between each kiss. Finally, she let out a moan as the elevator doors slid open with a *ding.*

They wasted no time to enter his apartment. As soon as the doors closed, he picked her up and they continued what they were doing. She wrapped her hands around his neck. He walked over to the big sofa in his living room, not even opening his eyes to get there.

He dropped her down and got on top of her. It was a big sofa, so they had ample space to mess around on it. While they made out, she slowly began the task of unbuttoning his shirt. Once the last one was done, only then did they stop to breathe again. She pulled it down his shoulders then off his arms.

She let out a soft 'mmm' when she saw how ripped his body was. Every woman loved a strong man, it just meant that he could protect them. It was one of those primal instincts within every person.

"You're so fucking sexy," he said between kisses down her body. He pulled her tight dress up from her thighs and she spread her legs in response. He nibbled on her soft flesh, making sure not to hurt her too much. When he was lower and he was face to face with her panties, he admired them. A white thong. Simple, yet elegant. She had a wet spot right where her hole was, revealing her pink lips beneath. He kissed her mound, working his way down. Her smell was sweet and musky.

He pulled the panties to the side and dug his face in. Sabrina was freshly shaven – she went into this knowing they would be fucking by the end of it. His cock was rock hard as soon as he licked her pussy – she was so soft, so wet. So slick.

She grabbed a pillow to her right and moaned loudly as he used the tip of his tongue to flick at her clit. He reached one hand up to fondle her breasts over her clothes, the other hand, preparing to slip inside of her.

He slid two fingers into her. Guided by how tight her walls became when he did something with his tongue, he found the perfect rhythm and intensity in which to work his magic. In no time, her walls pulsated around his fingers and she came with a high pitched, boisterous moan.

Satisfied with his work, he wiped the wetness from his face and started unbuckling his belt, ready to fuck her. She propped herself up on her elbows, then looked at him with a frown.

"Do you have a condom?" she asked.

Fuck.

He hoped she wouldn't ask and that she was on birth control instead.

Mason didn't typically like using them unless absolutely necessary. He was cut, so he lost a lot of sensation by wearing one. He felt himself going soft at the thought of having to wear a rubber. Nothing compared to fucking a woman raw. But he wouldn't be a dickhead and not do it. He still wanted to fuck her anyway. At least he'd last longer this time.

"Yeah! Sure, of course. Just caught up in the heat of the moment. Uh, I'll go grab it," he said.

"Thank you, Mason. Thanks for not being weird about it. I didn't want to ruin the moment or anything. I'm sorry," she said, likely noticing his facial expression had dropped.

Mason bent over her and kissed her on the lips. He wouldn't let this ruin the great night they had already had.

"Of course, sexy. It's just to be safe. Don't you worry your tight little ass," he whispered.

She giggled in response.

Mason rushed off to his bedroom to search for one. He hadn't used a rubber in so long that he had forgotten where he kept them. He checked the ensuite bathroom, thinking that was one of the places he was bound to have put it in. There was nothing there. He rummaged through the room, not finding it anywhere.

"Everything okay in there?" she shouted from the living room.

"Yes! All good. Be there now," he said back.

Finally, he found it in the drawer, the one that wasn't on the side of his bed. It was hidden underneath a book. Thank god, he thought.

He turned around, she stood in the door frame with one hand holding it. She was just in her bra and panties now. He just stared at her a moment, then grunted. Fuck, she was sexy.

"Hey, big boy. Sounded like you needed a little help in here," she said seductively. She looked around at the mess he had made in the room by rummaging through everything.

"Heh, got it in the end!" he said.

"Good. I want to fuck you, Mason. I want to fuck you so hard," she said.

He admired her body. She was small and thin, but looking much better without her clothes on. Although her breasts weren't massive, they were big enough to have perfect cleavage in the matching white bra she was wearing. She walked over to him and he sat down on the bed, the condom sitting next to him. He glared down at the condom. He really wasn't looking forward to wearing it. Made him feel like a dumb teenager all over again, it made him remember how he used to nervously fumble with it and forget to put it on. At least, as he got older, he learned how to find the right size and all.

She kneeled between his legs, finishing the job of taking his pants off. He lifted his ass to help her remove them. His massive cock sprung out from beneath the fabric of his boxers as she removed those too.

Her mouth fell open and her eyes widened at the sheer size of it. They always reacted that way. He nearly chuckled, but stopped himself.

"I – I," she took his cock in her small hands, hardly able to wrap her fist around it, "I don't know if I'll even be able to fit this in my mouth, let alone my pussy."

"We'll just have to try, right?" he said.

"Oh yeah," she moaned, "Yeah, we will definitely have to try."

She sat on her haunches to bring her face closer to his cock. Steadily, she stroked his cock while she prepared to take him in her mouth. She licked from the base, to the tip of his cock. He grunted as her wet tongue ran along his frenulum. Her tongue circled round the tip of his penis a few times, before she pursed her lips and slowly slid her lips over it.

He grunted.

"Fuck. It's been long," he said to himself.

She slid her lips lower and lower, her mouth being forced open wide. She gagged before she could reach half of the way down. It made him smile how much she struggled to fit him inside of her.

He laced his fingers in her hair, lifting and dipping her head down on his cock. He was slow and gentle – he didn't want to be as rough as he usually was. He stopped before she could gag each time before lifting her head up.

He wanted more though. It wasn't good enough.

It felt so good. So, fucking good.

As though possessed by something else, he began face fucking her with a ferocity she didn't seem used to. She gagged and groaned. He didn't stop when she started slapping his leg for him to slow down.

He carried on fucking her, staring down at her teary eyes and enjoying her suffering.

She had had enough, though, and pulled away from him even though his grip was so tight. She took a moment to catch her breath. She wiped the tears from her eyes. Seemingly deciding to let his force slide, she took the condom wrapper, tore it open. She pinched the tip of it, then slid it down his cock. She stroked his cock a few times, making sure it was secure. She crawled on top of him.

She firmly gripped his cock and guided him inside of her. She moaned loud, putting her hands on his chest to keep herself steady. She lifted and lowered herself down onto him repeatedly. She was having fun riding him, but he looked off to the side.

It wasn't really doing it for him. Not really. But he'd let her have her fun and be satisfied.

As she dropped down her small frame on him, she'd grind up against him, stimulating her clit against his pubic bone.

"Oh, god, oh god, yes," she screamed, "I'm gonna come."

Snapped back to reality, he looked back at her and thrust up into her as her walls tightened and relaxed around him. Finally, some sensation. This set him into a frenzy. He sat up, picked her off of him and pushed her onto her knees on the bed so her ass was facing him. She giggled at the sudden change of position. She was on her hands and knees, but that was not the way he preferred it.

So, he pushed her lower body down, so her face was against the bed. For a moment, he considered taking the condom off. But she'd notice. Besides, that would be kind of creepy.

"Mmmm, that was incredible," she said, "Your cock took some getting used to, but I'm hooked."

"Of course you got used to my cock, slut," he said softly.

"Sorry, what was that?" she asked. She looked back around at him and frowned.

"Oh, I just said of course you did, Sabrina," he lied.

"Oh," she said.

She put her head back down on the bed and waved her ass from left to right, anticipating his cock.

He got onto his knees on the bed, gripping her ass. His cock stood tall and hard, he didn't even need to hold it to guide it inside of her. She moaned as he slowly slid inside of her.

"Oh god, that hurts," she moaned, "Please go slow."

The few brief moments that he wasn't inside of her must have caused her tight walls to not be used to his sheer size anymore. It made him feel strong and incredible.

He did go slow, as she requested.
But he got bored again.
This was just plain old fucking.
It was boring.
If he wanted that he'd get married to someone who didn't love him.

She moaned and enjoyed herself. Slowly, sneakily, he increased the pace, hoping she'd just get used to it. He liked it rough. He liked it hard. She would too.

He increased the pace. She felt incredible. So tight and so small. His hands were so big against her small body. So easy for him to dominate.

He fucked her harder, each time his balls smacked against her thighs, she let out a loud grunt. He fucked her in a way every woman wanted to be fucked at some point.

He enjoyed this more, but he wanted more. He pushed all the promises he made to himself away. She was propped up onto her arms again, looking back at him as he fucked her. He lifted a leg, putting his foot on the back of her head, making her arms collapse beneath her, forcing her face into the sheets.

With his foot on the back of her neck, she couldn't move. He pulled her ass higher into the air, shifting himself higher above her. He pumped down into her harder than before, her loud moans muffled in the blankets of his bed.

"Ah, fuck," she moaned, "Stop, stop, you're hitting my cervix."

"Shut up, slut," he barked.

He fucked her even harder, letting out loud grunts continuously.

"Please," she begged, "Please."

She tried to move her head but couldn't with how hard his foot was forcing her down.

She kicked her legs at him, slapping him with her hands, trying to get free. He enjoyed her fighting, and didn't stop. In the scuffle, she became free, but ended up underneath him, staring up at him with her hands pinned on either side of her head.

"just stop when I say stop, okay?" she asked.

"Yes, I'm sorry. I just – I just get carried away," he said, "I'm sorry, sweetheart."

"It's okay," she said, she smiled at him.

"Do you want to carry on?" he asked.

"Yes, please. I want you to cum too, Mason. I've already come like three times," she laughed, "I came when we were in the elevator."

"In the elevator? Damn, I'm really good."

"Shut up and fuck me," she said. She bit her lip.

He put both of her wrists on one hand, with the other, he lifted and spread her legs for him.

"What a beautiful cunt you have," he said. It was a perfect, puffy pink pussy.

He thrust into her without hesitation.

He didn't go slow this time. He was done accommodating to her. He wanted his release now – he'd been anticipating it for days, saving himself just for her.

His free hand fondled her perfectly small breasts, pinching and squeezing her small nipples. They grew red from all the touching. She had her head bent backwards, her eyes rolled to the back of her head.

Her beautiful, pale and bare neck practically begged to be choked. He put it against her neck, only holding it at first. He felt his cock throb once he did. This was exactly what he needed to reach climax soon enough, even despite the condom.

He squeezed either side of her small neck, making sure not to press down on her windpipe.

He grunted as heat spread all throughout him and he was *almost there*.

Mason squeezed harder, her chest becoming flushed and her face too.

She pulled at his wrist, trying to get him away.

But he squeezed even harder.

"Stop," she croaked, "Stop. That's too hard."

"No," he grunted, "I won't stop, whore."

"Please," she begged. Her begging made his cock twitch. "Just let go."

His legs shook, his balls spasmed. He came with three more hard and deep thrusts.

As soon as she let go, she scurried backwards, away from him. She looked scared.

"What the fuck is wrong with you!?" she screamed, "I told you to stop. I could let the first time slid because you know, I was fucking horny. But then you choked me and didn't let go?"

"Listen, I didn't mean to hurt you," Mason said, "I had a really good time with you today. I just, I just get carried away."

Mason approached her to touch her shoulder reassuringly. She recoiled at his touch, slapping his hand away.

"Don't fucking touch me! You don't do that, Mason! You're a nice guy. I had such a good time at the restaurant. But you don't understand what no or stop means. You understand how fucking fucked up that is, right?" she shouted.

She rushed around the room, gathering her things, pulled her panties and bra on.

"No, no. That's not who I am – I swear, I just, I just get -" he started.

"Don't fucking tell me that you get carried away. Have some self-control, you piece of shit!"

She left the room, grabbed her handbag and made her way to the door.

"Please, let's just talk about this. I'm sorry," Mason pleaded.

"No. Fuck you and don't ever contact me again."

She left the apartment in her bra and panties, storming off and out of the building.

"Fuck!" Mason screamed, knocking a small vase off of the table.

He had done it again. He had fucked up again.

He hated himself for it.

Mason and Sabrina could have had something so good and so sweet, but he fucked it up, just how he had fucked up every other relationship in his life.

Shamefully, he removed the condom, tied it off, and chucked it in the bin. He had a shower, all the while feeling empty.

He felt like giving up. No one liked the way he fucked them, and he went too far *every single time.*

***

Sabrina blocked him on everything, and he never heard from her since. He spent the next few weeks burying himself in his work, distracting himself from the negative feelings. Just like he did every time this happened.

But, as the cycle usually went, he went straight back to the dating app, hoping that someone would come to accept him. He wasn't actually a monster, right? He just didn't go about things the right way. Fear and hesitancy stopped him from bringing up his tendencies when he first started speaking to someone. How would he bring that up, anyway?

"Hey, I like to choke and fuck someone so hard that they beg me to stop."

He couldn't just do that. It wasn't right. They'd run for the hills and never speak to him again.

Straight back to the app he went, though, but something inside of him wanted to do things differently. He set the age range between his, and fifty. Usually, he'd have it between twenty-five and twenty-seven, but maybe someone a year older would work.

Who knows.

Maybe that was what he was missing all along. Maybe that one woman that was right for him was just behind the surface of that age range.

He set his phone down and went about his day. His phone buzzed and he checked it.

He had matched with an oddly familiar woman. He remembered her eyes, those bright blue eyes.

The Seductress from the cocktail lounge. He couldn't believe his eyes. Could it really be her?

Her name was Scarlett.

"How fitting," he thought.

The age on her profile said she was forty-five, which took his breath away. She looked incredible for her age. She was eighteen years his senior, but he wanted to fuck her anyway.

He'd never been with a woman older than him before…

She sent a message first.

"Hey, you," she said, "You're the one from the bar. Your name's Mason? I like it."

He replied: "And your name is Scarlett. I like it too."

"So, what's a young man on you doing on this side of the world?"

"Trying new things, I guess."

"I'm guessing things didn't work out with that date of yours?"

"Yeah… Things kind of fell flat with that. Long story."

"Well, not to be a bitch, but I'm glad she's not in the picture. You really piqued my interest that night, Mason, and I am glad I can have a chance to have you all to myself."

"Hmm. Not bitchy. That's flattering, Scarlett. Where abouts do you live?"

"Literally a fifteen-minute walking distance from the bar," she said.

"Oh. Well, isn't that convenient. How did it go with the guy you took home?"

"Meh. He came in like five minutes, so I kicked him outta the house. Not dealing with that bullshit."

"Haha! Nice. Sorry to hear about him not pleasing you though. That's very unfortunate to hear."

"He didn't even bother to make me come first. He just couldn't wait to stick his dick inside of my pussy," she said.

He was at work and he had a hard on from only speaking to this woman for a few minutes. He looked around to make sure no one was watching, proceeding to adjust it underneath his waistline, in case he needed to stand up. He hovered over the 'send' button.

"I'd make sure you're fully satisfied before I even get my cock out, babe."

He decided to send it, to test the waters.

She replied instantly.

"Fuck. Now I'm wet. Listen, when I saw your profile on here, I had one thing on my mind and only one thing. That I want you to fuck me and have your every which way with me. You're tall, you're handsome, and I *know* you have a big fat cock in those pants of yours. Would you be up for that?"

"Are you sure you want to rush into things? I don't want to pressure you into having sex so soon. You don't want to get to know each other first?"

"Oh, shut up. I know what I want, and it's you. I mean, don't you think it's fate that we found each other."

"Yeah, I suppose you're right," he replied.

"Oh, and I'm guessing this is also running through your head. No, I'm not married and I'm not cheating on my husband. I got divorced like ten years ago and my kids are already outta the house. So, we're all good on that front."

"I wasn't worried about that. I saw you didn't have a ring on. It was one of the first things I looked at when I saw you."

"So, you instantly thought about fucking me when you saw me for the first time, hmm?" she teased.

"Well, yes. Honestly, I did," he replied. A smile was slapped across his face the entire time they had the conversation.

"Well, I know it's a little early and all, but would you like to meet up today?" she asked.

He stared at her message for a while, wondering if it was a good idea. What if she didn't like him, just like everyone else? He knew how to control himself now. After Sabrina had left, he made a real, true vow to himself. He wouldn't do that ever again. No choking. No slapping. No shoving.

"I can take time off whenever, really," he replied.

"Right, then, meet me at my place," she sent a pin of her location, "In twenty minutes."

It was spontaneous, but he was into it. It excited him to the core.

He left the office, leaving the floor manager in charge for the day. He lied, saying there was a family emergency. They'd be able to handle a few hours alone.

His car purred loudly on the trip there. He stopped in front of her place. *Just* outside of the city, her neighborhood was more suburban than his. He stopped in front of her house. It was a Victorian era style house, the classic white-picket fence house wife styled house he'd expected.

She fit the part, honestly. With her hair, the way she dressed and all, she looked like a 1950's housewife, even though they were in the modern times. He found it charming.

Once he parked in the driveway, he made his way to the door. This was insane. His hands were sweating. He couldn't believe he just left work early for a forty-five-year-old woman he had only met *once.*

She opened the door instantly when he rang the doorbell.

"Well, hello there. I'm honestly surprised that you came," she said. Her southern drawl was charming, and it made his cock twitch. She had a smile on her face, her eyes scanning him up and down.

Her house was white and airy, full of light.

"Well, can't blame me, can you?" he chuckled.

"No, I cannot," she smiled.

She touched his tie, feeling the soft fabric between her fingers. She twirled the tie around her hand and pulled him into the house. He closed the door behind him as she led him through the house like a puppy on a leash.

The house was well decorated and clean as a whistle.

She led him to what he guessed was the master bedroom.

"Undress me," she demanded.

She wore a white dress with a zip on the back. He did as he was told, slowly touching her shoulder, kissing her neck.

He unzipped her dress and it fell to the floor with a *thud.*

She wore exactly the type of lingerie that he had pictured. High-waisted garter belt, leopard print panties and bra to match.

She turned around and he looked at her.

"Holy fuck," he breathed.

Her body was incredible.

As though it had been carved out of stone by the gods. She was fit, curvy, and her tits were huge, almost spilling out of her bra.

"You like it, dontcha?" she teased.

"You're so fucking sexy, Scarlett," he said.

"Well, then I want you to have your way with me."

Without thinking, he shoved her down onto the bed. He got on top of her. Keeping in mind her previous encounter, he fingered at her lips to find her clit, expertly rubbing at it. He didn't care that her red lipstick would get all over him, and went in for a kiss. He kissed her hard and rough. She had a bit of a bush, but her pussy lips were neatly trimmed.

He pleasured her until she reached climax at least three times, using his fingers and tongue in alternation.

"Hmmm, that was so good, big boy," she purred, "But now it's your turn to have your fun with me."

She pulled his suit jacket off and undressed him. She bit her lip when she saw his cock, then looked up at him. He was on his knees on the bed now.

"This is even bigger than I thought it would be," she whispered.

"Thank you."

She got on her hands and knees, having no hesitation in taking his entire length into her mouth and down her throat. When he was in her throat, she would occasionally pulsate the muscles of her throat around his girth, squeezing on his cock. Her ass bounced as she moved herself back and forth onto his cock. He didn't know what to focus on, her ass or her face, with make-up filled tears streaming down her face.

It felt incredible and unlike anything he had ever experienced before. He didn't even have to guide her in order for the face fucking to happen, she sucked him off ferociously, with determination.

"Fuck," he moaned. He couldn't take it anymore, if she carried on, he would come.

Somehow knowing this, she pulled away and got onto her back.

"Fuck me, big boy," she moaned, "I'm so very wet."

She spread her legs, subsequently her lips, to reveal her glistening wetness. This woman took his breath away.

He reminded himself not to ruin things by being too rough. He crawled between her smooth legs, slapping his cock against her clit. She giggled when he did that, but grabbed his cock and shoved it inside of her. Pangs of pleasure rushed all throughout him upon entering her. He had to focus intently on not coming instantly – he understood now why the guy she fucked weeks ago had come so quickly.

She was intense. Sexy. Seductive.

Mason would never be able to get enough of Scarlett, no matter how hard he tried.

He carefully slid his cock in and out of her, holding her legs for balance. She moaned softly, her big blue eyes staring up at him as he did. She pulled her bra down to reveal her bare breasts. With each soft and careful thrust, they bounced and moved. He couldn't keep his eyes off of them. He felt those instincts in him once more, his hand going for her throat. He stopped just before he reached it, hesitating.

He fondled her breasts instead.

She looked down at his hand, then up at him.

Gripping his wrist, she pulled his hand up to her throat, then secured it around it. She gave him a reassuring nod. He squeezed, prompting a moan from her. He squeezed harder and her eyes rolled to the back of her head.

He fucked her harder while he choked her. She came on his cock, and he put both hands around her neck for stability as he had his way with her body. He grunted with each thrust. She was so wet and so tight, her pussy squeezing onto him with all its might.

"Was she...was she actually enjoying this?" he asked himself.

He pulled his hands away and shook his head. He didn't want to go too far. She chuckled through her gasping breaths.

"Why'd you stop, Mason? Didn't you like that?" she asked.

"No. I'm sorry. I shouldn't do that. It's fine," he said. He pulled out of her.

"What's wrong?" she asked, genuinely concerned.

"I shouldn't do that. It's not right. It's not right."

"Well, you seemed to like it, Mason." She glared at him.

"No. I shouldn't hurt women like that. I'm a monster," he admitted.

"Slap me."

She nudged him. She stroked his cock, it was slick with her pussy juices.

"No. I can't do that. I can't hurt you like that."

"Slap me, you fucking pussy."

He moaned as her hand masterfully jerked him off.

"Come on, you fucking coward. Hit me. Slap me. Fuck me like I'm some toy. Or are you too scared?" she demeaned him.

He snapped. He'd had enough.

"Shut the fuck up, whore," he spat.

He swung his hand at her face. Her cheek glowed red instantly. She didn't cry or tell him to stop, but instead, she moaned. He entered her again, but this time, fucked her with vigor.

"That's more like it," she moaned, "Do it again. Hit me. Fuck me hard. Hit me."

He did it again and again, slapping her across the face, then back handing her in the other direction while he fucked her. He could tell she enjoyed it – the muscles of her cunt pulsed with pleasure each time he struck her.

His hands were around her neck again when he was close to climax, the primal side of him taking over. She moaned uncontrollably by this point, and arched her back as he was about to climax. His legs shook, his entire body filled with ecstasy, as he shot his load inside of her. He was so drained by all the pleasure, in a good way, that all he could do was collapse on top of her. Scarlett let out a satisfied laugh, and wrapped her arms around him. He did the same.

He rolled over and lit a cigarette, and so did she.

The first intense, truly satisfying orgasm he had ever had came from a MILF.

The Living Doll

A tall woman sat on a chair within a massive, lavish living room, as though she had been put on display as a living work of art. The rest of the house fit the part, too, with large rooms and a frivolous number of windows. Her arms were tied behind her with a thick hemp rope. It dug into her skin but not enough to cut circulation. She could hear her heartbeat, it was so loud that it was the only thing she could focus on. Her legs were spread, each ankle tied to the legs of the chair. She wore a sexy, form fitting dress in the color red. It matched the red lipstick on her lips. The dress rode up her thighs, almost showing what she wore underneath said dress.

Today was a very important day and she tingled with anticipation for what would unfold. She was already wet, a wet spot forming in the seat of her chair. She had been tied to this chair since the last few minutes of sunlight and it was already pitch black outside now. The house was empty and quiet.

Her thoughts were interrupted by her husband kissing the top of her blonde head. It sent shivers down her spine.

"Hey, Stacy," he said. He sat in front of her, her chair was facing the three-seater sofa. The coffee table was to her left, moved out of the way to make space for her chair. There was another couch to her right, too.

"Hi," she said softly. Although she was bound, she wanted to reach out and touch his face. She was overwhelmed with arousal and love for her husband. She couldn't, of course and just tugged at the ropes that bound her wrists.

"Are you ready for tonight?" he asked.

"As nervous as I am, I am teeming with anticipation. My hands can't shake if they're bound, right?" she giggled.

"Mmmm, seeing you all helpless like this is giving me such a hard on, but I will wait. I should be patient, considering what will happen for the rest of tonight," he said.

"I'm ready."

"Good."

Her husband left the room and came back in with a big box in his hands. Slowly, he began unpacking its contents onto the coffee table next to her. Various vibrators, especially of the wand kind, dildos, and butt plugs were put down onto a small towel on the table. Next, he put down various whips and paddles. Some with long leather strands, a horse whip and her least favorite: a rubber paddle.

Next, he put down a variety of ball gags. A red one with a ball, one shaped like a ball for her to bite on, and another with a small dick shape, that would go into her mouth and cause major discomfort. BDSM wax candles. A lighter. More rope. Permanent markers. Lube. Cuffs. Lastly, he put down a pair of sharp scissors.

Her husband had prepared for absolutely everything he could have possibly thought would be useful. An overwhelming heat was forming between her legs and she hoped it would start soon. She really, truly couldn't wait for it to start.

"Which gag would you like for this evening, Madame?" he asked, speaking in a knock-off hoity-toity accent.

She giggled like a little schoolgirl.

"Hmm, sir, I would like whichever one you'd like," she replied in the same accent.

A sly smile formed on his face. He picked up the dildo gag and she inhaled sharply. Of course, he was going to torture with this one…

First, he gave her some water to hydrate before she wore the gag for who knows how long.

"Open wide, sunshine," he commanded.

She did as she was told. Slowly, he slid it into her mouth, and it filled her up. Her mouth was forced wide open by the short but thick instrument. He pulled it tight before strapping it in and securing it. Already, she felt saliva forming in her mouth from being forced to such an awkward angle.

He left the room again. From behind her, she could hear a loud grunt as he placed what he called

The Fuck Bench down on the ground. It was one of her favorite contraptions, with countless straps to hold her in place, forcing her into the doggy style position. He had spent months trying to build it and was very proud upon its completion. Her hands and legs would each have two straps, along with one that went around her waist, and another that would go around her neck, keeping her snug and in place. Most importantly, she would neither be able to move nor be able to stop anything that happened to her.

She couldn't wait to be put inside of it. Seeing all the toys and instruments before her made her all the more excited for what was to come. He kissed her on the head one last time, before he prepared some other things unrelated to her.

She stared at the clock on the wall across from her. As soon as it struck 09:00 p.m., people started arriving. One by one, her husband greeted them. Some of them, he hugged and others he shook the hands of.

Some were old friends and others were distant acquaintances. His best friend and that best friend's wife arrived last. No one seemed to notice her as he did the usual, showing them around the house and letting them know where they could get drinks and snacks if they needed.

Time went by and the drinks were flowing. It was a normal, everyday house party, barring the twenty-something year old sitting in the living room, tied to a chair. Some familiar faces played beer pong, occasionally cheering in excitement when they won the game. There were many different men and women from different backgrounds and walks of life.

Not once, throughout, had anyone acknowledged her presence. Saliva dripped down from her rose lips, causing a wet spot on her chest where it uncontrollably fell down. Although people hardly looked at her and she was so horribly ignored, she loved it. She felt so unimportant. So insignificant, while people had fun all around her. She would have smiled if it weren't for the gag in her mouth.

Finally, after an hour, Stacy received recognition. Her husband's best friend, Adam, came up to her with a drink in his hand. He inspected her, then chuckled.

"How are you liking this, slut?" he asked. His wife joined him, leaning on him. She had already had way too much to drink.

Stacy could only make a few dumb sounds in response.

"Good. Honey, would you like to do the honors?" Adam said. He looked over at his wife, Angie. Angie nodded excitedly.

"Yes! I'm so excited. Oh, my god," she beamed.

From the coffee table, she picked up the pair of scissors. The cold steel glistened in the well-lit room. She opened and closed it a few times, before sitting on her knees in front of Stacy. By now, a small crowd formed around Stacy. All eyes were on her. More and more people came as the blade came closer and closer to her.

Angie lined the scissor up between Stacy's legs, the stretchy fabric of her red dress nestled between the blades. She made the first snip, dragging the blade up her thighs, then her stomach. People watched intently as Stacy's body was slowly but surely revealed. The blades were cold against her skin as she came to her stomach. The fabric essentially sprung out of the way once it was freed of Stacy's plump breasts.

Once the large vertical cut was done, Angie cut it off of her shoulders, then pulled the fabric out from underneath her. She was in only her underwear now in front of some familiar and some strange faces. Her face glowed bright red, although the entire situation aroused her so greatly. Now, Stacy was only wearing a lacy set of bra and panties.

She wore a see-through bralette and her nipples were visible through the sheer fabric. Although so many eyes were on her she wasn't embarrassed about being nearly naked in front of all these people. The prying eyes from both the men and women made her feel sexy. She could see all of them mentally undressing her. She just couldn't wait for them to remove all the garments covering her skin.

Angie put the scissors down, when she sat back up, she started caressing Stacy's breasts. Through the fabric, she twisted Stacy's nipples.

"Take it off!" someone shouted from the back.

"Should I, baby?" Angie asked, looking up at her husband. With a smile on his face, he nodded at her.

Stacy snipped the bra off of her shoulders, then cut it in the center. It fell off to the side. Her clit throbbed when her bare breasts were on show for all to see. She couldn't wait anymore, she wanted someone to touch her. She wanted her release.

Next, her panties were pulled down. Angie stared down in delight at the wet spot in her panties.

"Look, everyone. The whore is wet," one of her old male friends said. They'd fucked once when she was about seventeen years old. She was surprised to see him here today. She grunted and moaned through the gag, begging for someone to touch her.

From a box to her left, her husband pulled out a pair of nipple clamps that were attached to a chain. He put them on both of her nipples, then stepped back and sat on the sofa in front of her. He watched as people played with her.

They tugged on the chain, pulling and twisting, bringing Stacy great pleasure. The added pressure of the clamps on her nipples as well as the pain brought her great pleasure. She let out a moan each time they were tugged at. They stimulated her sensitive nipples and once they were pulled off and the blood rushed back to them, she felt an intense pleasure wash over her once more.

A man she didn't recognize, one with dark raven hair, picked up a wand vibrator. He pressed a few buttons, testing out which one he'd prefer, before settling on the highest setting. He forced her legs closed, then shoved the vibrating toy between her legs. The vibrations brought her to climax almost instantly. All the teasing and the anticipation for the night had made her so excited that she couldn't hold on much longer to her next climax. Her knees were tied together so that she couldn't pull away to get relief from the intense stimulation between her legs.

While this happened, people wrote various derogatory remarks across her body.

Whore.
Slut.
Cum dumpster.
Sex doll.
Plaything.

She giggled when one of them wrote 'BIMBO' in big letters across her chest. By now, the chair she sat on was soaked from all the orgasms she had had.

Some men stroked their cocks through their pants as they watched her.

Other women had less shame about it and slipped their hands under their panties.

She was in pure, utter bliss.

It all became a blur at one point, her mind jumbled from all the pleasure she had felt. She didn't even notice when the restraints were cut from her knees and ankles, her legs forced wide open. A man with slicked back, blonde hair and strong, toned arms pulled her down so her ass was on the edge of the seat. He crouched down between her legs, putting each one over his shoulders. He buried his face in the wet sloppy mess that was her pussy.

The blonde man lapped up her juices, his tongue swirling around her soft lips. His tongue went as far as it could go inside of her and it felt incredible. His tongue fucked her for a while until he was satisfied, then he flicked his tongue against her clit. She dug the heels of her ankles into his back, hoping to get some relief for her uncontrollable shaking.

She arched her back as she came yet again.

The man stepped aside to let someone else have a turn. A short, curvy woman, picked up a long, girthy toy. She weighed it up in her hands before looking at Stacy with a sly smile. Stacy shook her head. She'd tried that toy before, and she could hardly fit an inch of it inside of her.

"You have no choice do you, whore?" the sultry woman said.

Stacy nodded. She really didn't have a choice in the matter.

Stacy put her feet up on the edge of the chair. The woman slicked the toy up with some lube, before rubbing it up against her lips. Slowly, she pushed the tip of the thick toy inside of her. There was a slight pain, but she adjusted to its size as soon its eight-inch length was inside of her. Slowly, the woman pulled it out of her, twisting and twirling it along the way. She looked up at Stacy to read her facial expression to make sure she was okay.

Stacy nodded at her and the woman smiled.

She fucked Stacy with the toy, slowly but surely increasing the pace of it.

What felt like hours went by, as people took turns having their way with her. They tested various toys on her, pushing her limits. Not once, though, did she want it to stop. She wanted all of it. Every inch of every toy, every vibration that came her way. She wanted it all and more. Although, she was missing something.

Not once, had anyone put their cocks inside of her. No one fucked her. No one *truly* had their way with her. To have her fantasy fulfilled, she needed people to fuck her. Every time she came, she starred her husband straight in the eye. She could tell that he was hard, and she wondered if he was uncomfortable at all, being hard for such a long time without release.

Her husband gave her a nod, before standing up and making his way over to Stacy. Her husband unbuckled the tight gag around her head. Slowly, he pulled it out of her mouth, a long strand of spit following behind. Her mouth felt almost numb from the gag being stuck in her mouth for so long. She moved her jaw left to right, hoping to get some relief.

He put his mouth to her ear.

"Are you ready, my baby?" he whispered.

"Yes," she whispered.

He made his way over to her, grabbing her chin firmly and forcing her to look him in the eye. He demanded a more respectful answer.

"Yes, I am ready, Master," she said proud and strong.

"Good slut," he said.

He stood before the crowd.

"Hello, everyone. I hope everyone has been having fun so far. Now, though, it's time for the real fun. Are you ready?" he said loudly.

In unison, everyone in the room toasted with their drinks in the air. All of them let out great, excited cheers for what was to come. The bounds around her wrists were released, giving her a sense of relief from the pressure. Although her gag was out now, she didn't say a thing. She wasn't allowed to speak yet.

She stood up. Instinctually, she covered her breasts with one hand and her crotch with the other. Her breasts spilled out from underneath her hand. Her legs weak and shaky as her husband led her over to The Fuck Bench.

Roughly, he ,shoved her down onto it. Diligently, she settled her knees on the padded rests that spread her thighs apart. He buckled both of her legs in, one around each calf and one around each ankle.

She settled her elbows on the padded armrests. Her lower arms laid flat. Again, they were tied down with two restraints. She tugged on them with her arms and legs, making sure that she was secure. They didn't budge.

Her face was shoved down into a hole in the bench, forcing her to stare down at the floor. He wrapped the strap around the back of her neck. She wouldn't be able to see who, or what they would be doing to her. Her ass was straight in the air, on display for the entire room to see. She smiled down at the floor. Finally, she would have what she wanted.

People demeaned her, throwing insults at her and spitting at her. They called her a filthy slut, making her feel an intense tingle between her legs. She loved being humiliated, especially in front of a crowd. She worked in such a high intensity field, having to be so serious and professional at all times.

She had to take care of her business image at all costs, lest she lose her reputation.

This was why she loved being treated like utter filth – it provided relief to her. Due to all the hustle and bustle of life and the high intensity of it, she liked to be treated this way. It made her feel less stressed and most of all, most satisfied.

Abruptly, a whip cracked against her big ass. It didn't stop as the person doing it swung against her, lifting their arm left and right as they struck her. She didn't groan out in pain, though, she moaned in delight. Squealed in ecstasy. Even when the rubber paddle hit her already red flesh, she loved it. As much as it hurt, it just added on to her pleasure.

The lashings stopped, and suddenly, she felt a cock slapping against her pussy. She was still as sopping wet as before. The slick skin of his cock rubbed against her with ease. Her ass was grabbed firmly, helping him guide himself inside of her. She wasn't sure exactly how big he was, but he was definitely girthy and filled her right up. He slipped in and out of her soft, wet cunt. He took his time with her body, relishing in every aspect of it.

She loved that she didn't even know who was fucking her right now. He pulled out of her, finishing himself off on her ass. The hot, sloppy liquid messed all over her backside. She giggled in delight. He didn't last very long or fuck her very hard to reach climax but she loved that. It made her feel sexy, desirable. One of the highest compliments a man could give in the bedroom was ejaculating so quickly because he enjoyed her body so intensely.

Man after man had his way with her, spraying his hot liquid all over her. It dripped down her curvy body, falling down onto the floor. Even the women had their own fun with her, prying and prodding at her body with their fingers, even using various toys on her. The women were more skillful at rubbing their clits – they knew exactly how to pleasure her. That was something she especially enjoyed about being with a woman. Despite this, there was nothing quite like cock. Not even big dildos could compare to Stacy's love for cock.

She had forgotten how many people had fucked her. Each and every encounter blurred into the other. She couldn't look at the clock anymore to tell the time, so she had no idea how long it had been.

Despite being so used and abused, she couldn't get enough of it even if she tried. She couldn't think about anything else but cock and cum. She was truly consumed by her carnal desire.

A warm cloth wiped away the excess ejaculate on her body.

Familiar hands touched her thighs. She knew who it was instantly as he shoved his cock inside of her. She could tell by the length and girth, the slight curve of his cock to the left. Her husband was behind her. She relished in the relief of knowing it was him.

As fun as the night was, she wanted her husband to fuck her too.

He slid himself in and out of her while the crowd watched. He didn't fuck her hard at all. Cold steel touched the delicate skin of her asshole – daring to breach inside of her. The lubricated, metal butt plug was plunged inside of her. She let out a shriek of delight. She felt so full now, having a cock inside of her pussy and a plug inside of her ass. His cock hardened up inside of her even more than before.

He was rock hard.

He took his time with her, experiencing her fully. He put a Hitachi wand into a slot in the contraption she was strapped to and secured it into place. As soon as the vibe was turned on, her walls tightened around his cock immediately, almost so much that it made it difficult to fuck her. He took this as a sign to fuck her even harder. Her husband pumped in and out of her doggedly. He stopped suddenly, before pulling out, then shoving back in the butt plug a few times. Stacy moaned out loud. She had no shame at this point. She moaned loudly without fear of sounding weird or lame. All throughout, she hadn't forgotten that people's eyes were on her.

Moans from various men and women came from the sofas. People had started fucking because they couldn't take the arousal without release anymore. Her moans mixed in with the others as he fucked her ass with the butt plug, loosening up her hole.

When he was satisfied, he tossed it aside.

She gasped when she felt the slick head of his cock rub against her asshole. He didn't wait to shove it inside of her, though. He didn't care to take it slow now. He wanted to fuck her ass and he wanted to fuck it now.

She could count every single inch of his cock sliding in and out of her. For the first time tonight, this was too much to handle. With the vibe on her clit and the people watching her and her husband fucking her ass so intensely, she couldn't feel her limbs anymore. She didn't tell him to stop, even though it was too much because she was in two worlds divided.

It was too much.

But she couldn't let it stop.

She wanted him to come inside of her. He was the only person in the world that was allowed to do it – because she was *his*.

Stacy's husband smacked her ass a few times, making it jiggle. She felt no more of that familiar pain that came with anal. Only pleasure. She came three times already by the time he was close. She could tell by his increasing pace and loud grunts – that was the only time he moaned that loud during sex: when he was near climax.

His pace slowed and he thrust into her hard.

His hot come filled her ass up. When he pulled out, it leaked out of her ass, flowing down her lips and dripping onto the floor.

Stacy was happier than she had ever been.

The room got quieter and quieter as her husband rounded everyone out.

"Alright, everyone, it's time to go. My beautiful wife needs some rest. I hope you enjoyed the show. We'll inform you when she is ready to do this again," he said.

Some disappointed groans came from the crowd, but they left anyway.

Angie came over to her.

"Hey, honey. I hope I wasn't too rough on ya. Brunch on Sunday as usual, alright?" Angie said.

Stacy couldn't reply. She couldn't speak or make a sound. She had lost her voice from all the moaning she had done through the night. Angie grabbed Stacy's hand and squeezed; Stacy squeezed back. She seemed to understand and walked off. A few minutes went by as her husband sent everyone off on their way. He cleaned up the mess their guests had made, making sure everything was spotless before unstrapping his wife.

She was glad her husband anally fucking her was the last event of the night. She couldn't feel her legs anymore. Now that she wasn't receiving any stimulation and no one was fucking her, she realized how fragile and sore she felt. She was raw. Her ass stung from all the spankings. Her pussy lips were swollen from all the friction. She was covered in permanent marker and her red lipstick was practically smudged all over her face.

She felt a sense of relief wash over her when all her restraints were untied. He had a silk gown in hand already and wrapped it around her. They walked off together to their massive en-suite bathroom. He sat her down on the edge of their large, hot tub style bathtub. He turned the tap on and started filling it up with water and bubbles.

He removed her gown as well as his own clothes, then hopped in with her. She sat in between his legs with her back to him. Since the bathtub was so big, it allowed for him to lay back with her in his arms. They laid together in the hot water for a while, before he began scrubbing her back, washing her hair and then her face. He gently scrubbed away at the hurtful words on her skin. Luckily, they disappeared with ease.

She was quiet, but not because she was upset. She loved that about him: he didn't care to fill up silence with meaningless small talk. He was okay with things being quiet when they needed to be. He nurtured and cared for her. He held her tight against her body.

When their fingers and toes became too wrinkly, they got out of the bath. He wrapped a towel around her. She felt better after the warm bath – it soothed all her raw and aching bits.

"I laid out some pajamas for you, baby," he said, "They're on the bed."

She pulled on the pajamas. It was her favorite pair. Pink, fluffy and decorated with cute little sheep. They got into bed and she sighed happily when she was under the sheets, in the love of her life's arms.

The first real words she uttered in hours were: "That was incredible, honey. Thank you so much."

No Means Yes

The shots were flowing, and Aubrey was having a good time. It was difficult to keep up with friends in her late twenties, considering that everyone had work and their own lives to take care of. So, they made a promise to one another that they would meet up at least once a month to have some drinks and catch up on how life was going. Aubrey was in charge of fetching drinks from the bar this evening, so she got her friend's orders and made her way to the bar. They had their backs to her and were distracted by each other's conversation.

"Hey, can I have four shots of tequila and four beers please," she asked. It had been a good night, she needed this night with her friends. Life had been particularly difficult as of late and she needed the down time. Life was demanding and it was good to let go of that sometimes and just pretend that everything was okay.

The bartender did his thing and started preparing her drinks, handing them to her, one after the other. Suddenly, she felt the presence of someone that was standing a little too close to her for comfort. A hand groped her ass and squeezed hard. She spun around to see who it was, and she slapped the hand away.

"Don't touch me!" she said loud and firm.

The man undressed her with his eyes before looking up at her face. His hand moved up to touch her breast. Unlike before, she didn't respond in anger. She just froze in place, unable to move. Her muscle and bone petrified her in place. He touched her breast, squeezing hard, so hard it hurt. All she could do was shake her head at him. Words wouldn't escape her lips and she couldn't scream.

The man looked down at her body, his hand slowly running down her waist. The bartender finally stepped in when the man was just about to slip his hand under her dress and fondle with her panties. Aubrey felt violated and she couldn't do anything about it. She felt pathetic for having frozen up and needing someone else to stop this from happening.

"Is everything okay over here, ma'am?" the young bartender said.

Aubrey shook her head again.

"Is he giving you problems?" he interrogated.

"I don't know who this man is," Aubrey finally said.

"Come on, baby. I'm just having a little fun. It's harmless," he said. He was handsome, with a sexy five o'clock shadow, so his actions didn't remotely suit his looks. She would have expected to be groped by a greasy old man, not a handsome man around her own age.

"Sir, you're making her uncomfortable. It would be best for you to leave before things get too messy," the bartender said.

"Come on, can you blame me? Look at what she's wearing," he said. He gestured to her little black dress that was short enough to reveal all if she bent over.

"Sir, I won't say it again. Leave, now. I won't be serving you tonight," the bartender said.

"Fuck, fine. I'll leave. I was just having a little fun, I wasn't trying to start any fights," the man said. He took his broody eyes and dark hair and left the bar.

"Sorry about that, I – I don't know what to do in those situations," Aubrey said. She smiled at the bartender that saved her.

"There's no reason to say sorry. That wasn't your fault at all. These drinks are on me. We try and keep the creeps out of here, but you know how it is," he said. The tall, young man proffered the drinks over to her.

"I can't do that, please, I really don't mind. Let me pay," Aubrey insisted.

"No, ma'am. It's the least I can do for your troubles," he said.

Aubrey huffed and took the drinks to the table. Her friends welcomed her with bright smiles as she put all the drinks down.

"What took you so long, Brie? Everything all right?" the red haired friend, Callista, asked.

"Oh, nothing. Just got held up at the bar," Aubrey lied.

"Well, drink up, ladies," the blonde-haired friend said. They all raised their tequilas into the air in toast and downed them quickly. Aubrey stifled a cough – she would never get used to the taste of tequila. It was just dreadful, and she didn't understand how people *liked* tequila.

They spoke of everything and nothing until their drinks were almost done. Their careers, their family, reminiscing on the past. It was a surprise they were all still friends after all this time. Aubrey had been friends with this group of girls since they were all in high school. They were coming up to ten years of friendship.

"So... I know that you don't like talking about this stuff, but you can't hold it in forever," Callista said, "How is it going with that guy, Aubrey? What's his name, Nicholas?"

"Oh, yeah. His name's Nick," Aubrey tucked a curl behind her ear, "It's going good, I guess. I don't really know what to say." Aubrey wasn't much of a fan of sharing her personal life details until she was sure things were right. It was a thing she lived by – she didn't share exciting news until she achieved said goal or aspiration. The same thing with relationships, she didn't like to share much about them until she was sure that the relationship would last.

"Come on, all of us shared our spicy lil details," Callista said, "Do you really not have any news at all?"

Aubrey rolled her eyes and huffed. "Fine. Okay, it's going well. We've only been together for a year but I kind of think he's the one, you know? Everything just feels right with him. He just gets me, you know?"

"Mmmm, well, a year's a long time when you consider our histories with dating," her friend pointed to all her other friends sitting around the table, "I mean, I feel like my longest relationship was four months."

"Heh, I suppose you're right. But yeah, he's good to me. But we're taking things slow and exploring each other as we go along," Aubrey said.

"Hmm, exploring each other? Is that a sex thing?" Callista asked.

"Shh, don't be obscene. I meant personality wise and stuff," Aubrey said. Her face flushed at the thought of their sexual escapades.

"Sure thing, sweetheart," Callista said with a sarcastic wink.

Aubrey felt dizzy and hot as she sipped on her last bit of beer for the night. She had had a good time with her friends at this dingy bar, but she knew it needed to come to an end soon. She had work in the morning so she couldn't let it go on for much longer. Usually, they'd stay until closing and be essentially kicked out of the pub, but she needed to be a responsible adult and get into bed early this evening. She paid her part of the tab and said goodbye to her friends. She was offered a lift, but decided to make the short walk home. She needed some fresh air. She hoped that by the time she reached her apartment building, she'd have sobered up at least a little bit.

She wasn't really much of a fan of drinking, she only really did it once a month when she saw her friends. She didn't really see the appeal in getting drunk at all. It would make her lose control of her inhibitions and she'd make a fool of herself. Besides, hangovers were terrible for her. They made her want to never drink again. Her least favorite, though, was when she got home after a long night of drinking and got into bed. That uncontrollable spinning feeling that washed over her made her feel sick. Aubrey loved her friends, but she hated that they couldn't have fun without having alcohol involved.

The night air was cold and crisp, just as she wanted it to be. Even through her thick coat, her nipples hardened against the soft fabric of her bra. The streets were quiet and empty, and she made the walk without looking up from the ground. She knew her neighborhood like the back of her hand because she liked taking walks so often. She could make the trip home with her eyes closed. She walked a few steps, the heels of her boots clicking with each step. She stopped in her tracks when she heard footsteps behind her. The footsteps stopped. She held her coat close to her chest, crossing her arms over it. Aubrey was sure she was just being paranoid, so she brushed it off.

She looked behind her and saw nothing but streetlamps and parked vehicles. There was no one in sight and no one behind her. Aubrey looked around one last time, just to be sure.

"Hello, is anyone there?" she said out loud.

There was no response. She hovered in place for a while before she turned back around to go home. She was only a few minutes away from the comfort of her bed. She increased the pace of her steps, but she still heard the same footsteps echoing her own. This time, though, she looked back, and saw a cloaked figure just a little bit behind her. She increased her pace into a run, hoping and praying that her feet didn't fail her. She tried to harness her skills learned in high school running competitions, steadying her breathing as she sprinted away.

She took a turn, hoping to throw off the person that was following her. She ran down the small alleyway, hoping to not slip. She had finally gained some hope in getting away from her potential attacker. She swore at herself for not taking the lift from her friend. She was terrified and scared for her life. She had already been harassed by a man earlier and now it was happening again. By sheer unluck, she had turned into a dead-end alleyway, forcing her to stop in her tracks. Her heart beat so heavy in her chest that she felt like she couldn't breathe, that she was going to die.

Just as she turned around to make a break for it back down the alleyway, she was met by a looming figure standing over her. Before she could react or defend herself, she was met with a white cloth to her mouth. An overwhelming sweet smell filled her nose. The tall, strong man wrapped himself behind her, keeping the cloth over her mouth. She tried pulling and tugging his hand away to no avail. She lost feeling in her arms and legs and couldn't fight back anymore. Everything went black from there, and she had a dreamless sleep. All was peaceful. All was black.

As she was knocked unconscious by chloroform, she collapsed in place. Her knees buckled and her eyes closed. The man caught her before she hit the ground. He put her over his shoulder and carried her quickly to his car which was nearby. He looked left and right, before walking into the street. Aubrey was half conscious by now, she could see what was going on, the ground appearing

and disappearing before her eyes, but she couldn't
move, and she couldn't speak. He opened the boot to
his car, then gently placed her within. When the boot
closed, she passed out.

***

Aubrey woke up when she hit her head on
something. She woke up in a jolt, trying to look
around and figure out where she was. She was in a
confined space and instantly overwhelmed by
claustrophobia. Her mind was still foggy, and she
felt nauseous. She tried hitting at the walls
surrounding her, but it didn't work. She was stuck.

Finally, she understood where she was and
what was happening, when she hit her head again.
She was in a moving vehicle and going over a bump
had caused her to hit her head. She wanted to scream,
but nothing came out. She tried with all her might,
but she knew it was futile. No one would hear her
and there was nothing she could do. She heard the
brakes come to a screeching stop. The sound of
footsteps came towards her, before the man spoke.

"If you scream, I'll fucking kill you," he said
firmly, "When I open the trunk, you will stay silent.
A single squeak and you're done. You got me?"

"Uh, huh," she whimpered.

"Say yes, I will stay silent," he barked.

"Yes, I will stay silent," she obeyed.

"Okay, I'm opening the trunk now. Be silent."

The trunk swung open. She tried to sit up and get out and try to make a run for it, but her muscles didn't obey. The masked man took a piece of cloth out of his pocket. He lifted her head and wrapped it around her head.

Applying pressure in a specific spot on her jaw, he forced her mouth open. He secured the cloth in her mouth, before tying it tightly on the back of her head. Aubrey dipped in and out of consciousness as he helped her out of the trunk, and picked her up once more. This time, he carried her like his bride. Like his very own prized possession. She wrapped her arms around his neck, and passed out again.

When she awoke, she was in a near dark room. Judging by the brick walls and the dampness of the air, she was in a basement. She felt like she had finally woken up properly by now and hoped that she had control of her limbs again. She scanned the room to try and see if there was a way out, but it was dimly lit, and her eyes hadn't adjusted yet. She tried to tug at her arms, but they were secured tightly behind her back. Her legs were spread and tied to the chair, too.

Aubrey had become accustomed to the heaviness of her beating heart by now, although it was the only thing she could hear. She tried making a noise and screaming at the top of her lungs, but the gag in her mouth stopped her. She let out a frustrated groan at how useless she felt. She would have loved to be able to be strong and kickass like the women in the movies, always with a plan B for every situation.

But Aubrey had nothing with no way out of her situation. She didn't have a knife. She couldn't move from the chair, it seemed to be secured to the floor. She was powerless. She hoped that this was all some sick, disgusting dream, and she was actually in her bed, comfortable, under her sheets.

She knew it wasn't a dream when the masked man made his way down the stairs, his heavy-booted steps echoing throughout the room. When he reached the bottom, he turned to face her. He had a black hoodie on, with matching black pants. When he stopped, he turned on a light, and it burned her eyes. It filled the room with a clinical, white light. She looked around, hoping to see something that would get her out of this, but the room was impeccable.

She was in the middle of the room, on a bolted down chair. On her left, there was a double bed with impeccable white sheets. In one corner, there was a bar fridge, and behind her, she saw a comfortable looking sofa.

The man made his way over to the bar fridge and fetched something from it. He walked over to her and crouched down.

"I'm going to remove the gag. You can scream if you want to, but no one will hear you. These walls are soundproof, and no one will ever hear you. Now, be a good girl and drink some water. The shit that knocked you out is going to give you a headache if you don't drink something," the man said. He spoke quickly, but with an assertive tone. Aubrey nodded at him enthusiastically. She stared at him, her eyes begging him to let her go.

He took his time untying her gag, as though to torture her even further. He chucked it into a laundry basket. He really had planned for everything, hadn't he?

As soon as the gag was free from her mouth, she finally mustered the strength to scream. She begged for help, she roared with determination to get out of her situation. The man watched her with his arms crossed over his chest, as though he was enjoying this. She screamed until her throat felt raw and she was out of breath.

Her kidnapper burst out laughing. A loud, thunderous, belly laugh filled the small room. It made her feel like utter shit. It was all for nothing. She thought that could have at least helped something, but he found it amusing! It made her angry, but her eyes filled with tears.

"Are you done?" he teased, "I told you no one can hear you. Scream until you lose your voice. No one's going to know and no one's going to care, bitch."

Aubrey nodded her head at him. "Yes."

He opened the bottle of water and brought it near her mouth. As much as she wanted to fight it, she lapped the entire bottle of water up like sweet honey. The cold liquid filled her up and made her realize how truly thirsty she was before.

He crushed the bottle until it was small and chucked it away.

"Thirsty, huh?" he asked.

Still crouched down in front of her, he looked up at her. He stroked her cheek, catching a stray tear along the way. Aubrey frowned at him as she saw his eyes admiring the rest of her body. She wasn't wearing the thick black coat anymore, only her small, tight black dress. The thought of the man touching her while she was knocked out made her feel sick.

The tips of his fingers trailed down from her cheek, to her neck, to her prominent collar bones. He touched the soft flesh near her cleavage, before moving to her shoulder. He slipped the strap off of each one of her shoulders. He was gentle and soft.

When he gripped the fabric that covered her breasts, she tried to pull away. The chair was firm and stable, and her protests were for nothing. Aubrey couldn't move away from him as he violently ripped down her dress, tearing it along the way. He let out a soft grunt when he saw her tits in her bra. She was wearing a matching set tonight, black and lace and leopard print.

She shouldn't have worn such nice lingerie tonight. It seemed to have sent him into a frenzy, and he ripped her bra down, revealing her small breasts.

"Fuck me," he said, "A lot smaller than I would have anticipated. So, you wear padded bras just to make your tits look bigger? That's pathetic."

Aubrey looked off to the side and didn't say anything. This angered him.

"I'm speaking to you, whore!" he demanded, "I asked you a question."

"No," she sobbed, "It's just comfortable. And it makes my boobs look good."

"Well, I don't see how the bra's practical."

"My tits aren't that small," she sobbed, "Why are you doing this? Please, just let me go. I haven't even seen your face and I don't know how I got here. If you just drop me off at my apartment and blindfold me, I won't be able to tell the cops anything to identify you."

He ignored her and started touching her breasts. His hands were cold to the touch and he squeezed her tits so hard it hurt. He took each nipple between his fingers and twisted and turned. She bit her lip and stifled a moan. Having smaller breasts meant that her nipples were more sensitive, so any kind of stimulation made her instantly wet. She hated her body's natural response to her nipples being played with, but she couldn't stop it. He crouched down between her legs, one hand playing with her breast.

He pulled the mask off of his face. His five o'clock shadow and broody eyes were familiar. She wanted to try and beg him to stop, but knowing who he was now, she knew he wouldn't. He wanted her and there was nothing she could do about it.

"There, you've seen my face. Now I can't let you go," he chuckled, "You're all mine now, bitch."

"Please stop," she begged, "There's no evidence of you doing anything. Even if I go to the cops, they wouldn't believe me because I don't have any bruises or anything and we haven't gone that far yet. Please, stop."

Again, he chuckled and ignored her pleas. He fondled one breast, and the other breast, he took into his mouth. His tongue flicked at and swirled around her nipple. Her breathing became heavier and heavier and she couldn't hold it in anymore. She let out a moan. A heat built up between her legs, along with an intense throbbing. He pinched and twisted her nipple while he sucked on the other. A wave of pleasure washed over her, sending an aching and pulsating feeling down into her crotch. As much as she wanted to fight it, her body felt great, so she couldn't. She was torn between wanting it to stop and wanting him to push her over the edge. The only thing she could use was her words to make it stop.

"S-stop," she whispered, "Please, stop. I'll d-do anything."

His blue eyes stared up at her and he smiled, the right side of his mouth tugging higher than the left.

"Beg harder, little one. And it's master, to you," he said.

"What?" she scoffed.

"You call me master when you refer to me or else you get punished."

"O-okay, Master," she whimpered, "Can you let me go now?"

"I'm going to untie you at some point but I'm not letting you go, stupid," he chuckled.

Aubrey whimpered as the pressure around her legs was relieved. He touched her leg, moving his hand up her inner thigh painfully slowly. She whimpered as the tips of his fingers touched up against her panties. He applied a bit of pressure before rubbing up and down her slit. He pulled his fingers away and showed them to her. His fingers glistened with her juices.

"You're wet," he scoffed, "You soaked my fingers, even through your panties. All I did was play with your nipples. Are you really that much of a sex starved slut that that made you feel so turned on?"

"I… My nipples are really sensitive, okay. I couldn't help it, I don't know what happened, I'm sorry."

He shook his head at her. "Tusk, tusk. I knew you were just a dumb slut. When's the last time you had sex?"

Aubrey paused for a moment to think of something to say. "I had sex on Wednesday," she paused for yet another moment, "I have a boyfriend and we have sex often."

"Hmm. So, I'm going to be taking the purity of a taken woman, then. Did you think that I'd be put off of this because you have a boyfriend?"

"No," she defended herself, "I was just being honest. We're here now, right? There's no way I can get out. Why should I lie to you?"

He grabbed her face, firmly holding her chin between his thumb and forefinger. It hurt and it dug into her skin, hurting her teeth through her gums. It was an unexpected move, and it made her whimper in fear.

"You're just trying to manipulate me into letting you go prematurely. A classic tactic you've probably seen in movies, right? Sweet talk your captor so they become weak and falter."

"No, no. I'm not doing that," she said, "I swear."

"Whatever you say, slut. You're mine now and I control you. You will do what I say, immediately. Do you understand that?"

"Yes, master."

He nodded at her before letting her go, throwing her face to the side. He removed his hoodie to reveal a white shirt tucked into his dark jeans. He rolled his sleeves up, all the while making eye contact with her. She caught glimpses of his ripped body. Through his shirt, she could see he was buff and looked after himself well. She was torn between being both disgusted by him and being attracted to him and it confused the hell out of her.

He stood in front of her and plunged his fingers inside of her without hesitation. She clenched her jaw as two of his fingers filled her up. She was especially tight today. She bit her lip to stifle her moans yet again, hoping to not make him think that she was enjoying this. What if he didn't like that? What if he beat her because he didn't like her enjoying it, since he could be getting kicks out of her for not being into what was happening?

He plunged his fingers deep into her pussy, applying pressure on her G-spot as he pulled his fingers out, repeating this action so many times that she felt she was close to orgasm. He looked into her brown eyes while he fingered her, and she didn't look away. She wasn't sure if it was out of fear or because she got lost in the deep pools of his irises.

He got especially invested in this act when she couldn't hold the moans in anymore, quickly moving his other hand over to rub her clit. She felt an intense pressure build up inside of her, and she screamed profanities out into the room. She was about to squirt. Clear liquid sprayed all over as she reached orgasm. Her head became foggy and she couldn't breathe.

That was the best orgasm of her life.

He pulled away from her, wiping his soaked hand on the back of his jeans. She sat there in a pool of her own juices, feeling defeated yet sexually satisfied. This man had won. She had come and that meant that she liked it.

He admired her for a moment. She was a mess. Bra tugged down to her waist, her tight dress pulled up there too. Her legs spread, panties pulled to the side, the seat soaked to the brim. He bent over her and fiddled with the rope behind her. Suddenly, he pulled her down and she slipped off the chair, landing firmly on the ground, her hands still tied behind her back. It was even more uncomfortable now that her hands were raised up slightly behind her.

She looked up at the tall man standing merely a few inches away from her. Master unzipped his jeans and pulled his cock out through the zipper. She gasped when she saw how monstrous his girth was.

She stared at his long cock a moment and looked up at him again with a frown.

"Suck my cock, slut. You're a cum crazed whore, but I know you're obsessed with dick just as much," he teased, "Come on, show me your skills."

Aubrey whined a little and opened her mouth. He inched his cock forward and grazed it against her lips. As the head came closer to her mouth, she realized that she needed to open her mouth even wider, almost so wide that it would hurt her jaw. She put her tongue out and licked at the sensitive, smooth skin of the tip of his member. She wrapped her lips around it, before sliding his length inside of her mouth.

She looked up at him as she did this and was surprised to find that she was only halfway there by the time he nudged at the back of her throat. She had no gag reflex, though, so he pushed down through her throat with ease. He let out a satisfied grunt when her lips touched the base of his cock and he was all the way inside of her mouth.

His eyes were full of lust for her. A deep, carnal lust that terrified her. How could one man want her so much?

He laced his fingers through her soft hair. Both of his hands gripped her head.

Just as she was about to pull away and continue giving him a blowjob, he held her firmly in place. At first, she accepted it, but she soon realized what he was doing. His cock was all the way down her throat, but he wasn't letting her free and she couldn't breathe. She tried pulling her head back as she tried gasping for air, but his cock blocked her air passage. She felt dizzy and her face started going red when he finally released her. She hyperventilated until she could finally feel normal again. Tears streamed down her face, but she persisted and took him into her mouth again.

He stretched her mouth wide open with his big cock, but she eventually got used to it as she started enjoying it. She let out a soft moan each time his cock reached the back of her throat, adding more sensation to it with the vibration of her moans. She noticed him gripping her hair tighter and tighter. He thrust into her mouth more vigorously and each time he thrust, he let out a grunt. He was close...

Despite being used by this man, her cunt was throbbing for more. She couldn't wait for him to shoot his load down her throat, but he pulled away. She whimpered unhappily. He tucked his cock back in his pants and walked behind her. Her makeup was messed up. Her mascara was messed up, making black lines that ran down from her eyes to her cheeks. Her lipstick was smeared and messy and she looked like a cheap whore.

He untied her wrists. She stayed still, not pulling her arms in front of her for a while. She was hesitant and careful in her actions, hoping to not set him off in anger now that she wasn't giving him pleasure, it meant he wasn't preoccupied, and could be angered easily. When she eventually did, she rubbed at her joints to get some relief. Her pale skin was red from being bound for so long and she wondered if there would be marks left on her skin from it.

Aubrey still sat on the ground. Her Master gripped her hair again. This time, he wasn't gentle and pulled her hair, guiding her to the bed on the other side of the room. She kicked and screamed as her legs dragged on the ground. She tried to gain some footing but was being dragged too fast. He pulled her up and threw her down onto the bed.

It was a nice fantasy, when she was sucking him off. But fucking him was different… Was she ready for it? He was so big, and it would definitely hurt…

He got on top of her and pulled his cock out again. He was harder than ever before. She tried closing her legs to stop him, but it didn't help, he was already between her legs and she was pinned.

"Stop fighting it," he barked, "Just let it happen. Your hands are pinned, and your legs are spread. You're already so wet… You want it so bad, don't you, bitch?"

"No. Please, I don't want to do this anymore. Please," Aubrey cried. Tears streamed down her face, they were real tears and weren't fun and games anymore. She was seriously crying.

For a moment, his expression changed. He softened up and he looked at her with concern. His grip on her wrists eased and he almost let go. She looked him in the eye and gave him a reassuring nod.

He cleared his throat softly, and he went back into his cruel, demeaning attitude. He gripped her wrists so hard that his fingernails dug into her skin. With his knees, he forced her legs to open wider. She tried wriggling away, but she was fully pinned by his body weight. With her dainty wrists pinned down with one of his hands, he stroked the tip of his cock over her slit and up to her clit.

Her Master did this so many times that she couldn't take it anymore. All he needed to do was apply some pressure and push himself inside of her and she would get what she wanted. By now, the tip of his cock was slick with her wetness. She tried lifting her hips when he brought his member close to her hole and teased it, hoping that it would slip inside.

And it did.

She arched her back and her eyes rolled to the back of her head. There was nothing more pleasurable in the world than when he slipped it inside of her for the first time, especially considering his monstrous side. She giggled in sheer glee and ecstasy. Her master buried his face in her neck while he fucked her, kissing her at first, but nibbling her eventually. She wasn't sure if he was biting hard or not because she was so filled with euphoria and pleasure. He could have drawn blood and she wouldn't know because his cock felt so good inside of her.

She could feel every thrust and every twitch so precisely, every movement in and out of her. It was almost overwhelming for her, that she couldn't take the pleasure anymore. He was so into fucking her that he eventually let go of her wrists and he pulled his face up to hers. He dove his head down and kissed her, while he touched her breasts. She moaned into his mouth occasionally while she kissed him back.

She was lost in the moment and forgot about every single worry in the world.

All she knew and all she wanted was this moment with him.

She felt so full and so warm and every fiber of her being was tingling with pleasure. The weight of his body on top of hers and the sheer helplessness she had felt just moments before was her favorite feeling in the whole world.

"I want you to cum inside of me," she whispered in his ear.

Upon her final word, he gripped her wrists again and fucked her violently. Her small tits bounced up and down and their moans and grunts were in unison. His cock twitched and he squirted his load inside of her. She moaned one last time and finally felt herself come back down to earth again.

He rolled over onto his back and she snuggled up into his arms. Aubrey let out a satisfied sigh and closed her eyes, getting a little bit of rest after the busy night.

"That was pretty fucking amazing for your first time, Nick. I love you. Oh my god, I love you so much and thank you for doing this for me," she said with the biggest smile on her face.

"No, thank you. That was definitely an interesting experience," he chuckled nervously, "I wasn't sure if I'd be into it when you brought it up, you know, it's kind of weird to put myself into the headspace of a kidnapper."

"Yeah, I understand, honey," she stroked his cheek, "But you did well, and I am happy, okay? You don't have to worry, we both know this is just a fantasy."

"Of course. Of course. I just want you to know I didn't mean any of the stuff I said, it was just an in the moment thing and I would never actually say any of that stuff to you. I love you, Aubrey."

"I will say though, what a brilliant idea to just bring it up unexpectedly on girls' night. It was so sexy. It's been my kink since I can remember, and no one's actually been willing to do this for me. So thank you, I am finally satisfied. Also, bolting the chair to the ground was such a smart move. Gave me real psycho vibes."

"That's why I haven't let you in the basement for a few weeks," he said.

He kissed her on the forehead and cuddled her for a while. They headed upstairs for a snack before having a shower and heading to bed, falling asleep in each other's arms. Aubrey, for what seemed like the first time in her life, was fully satisfied.

Mother's Boyfriend

Nicky, a timorous girl, just turned eighteen at the start of the year. She was in the last year of high school and couldn't wait to have it over with and move the hell away from it all. She was an adult now and she was so tired of dealing with studying, teachers, and especially the people in her school. She just didn't relate to them and she couldn't stand it anymore. She was planning to go through the year keeping her head down and doing what she needed to do in order to get through it. At least she had that to focus on, since her personal life was difficult.

Her father wasn't in the picture and hadn't been for years. He was an alcoholic and went too far with his drinking, so she had to move in with her mother who wasn't much better. Her mother was a junkie and couldn't hold a job for long, not to mention find a committed relationship that wasn't toxic. Nicky over the years, had to deal with so many of her mother's boyfriends who were crazy and controlling. Because of that, they never really stayed in one place for very long.

She was going through another one of these big life changes. Over the weekend, her mother and her packed all their things to leave an abusive household. Nicky and her mother, Elizabeth, had a place ready for them to move into. They left when he wasn't home, and they didn't look back. Nicky compartmentalized her feelings on the situation- or at least tried to.

Things were bad with Elizabeth and her partner for at least the past six months and as usual, it was time for them to run away from a bad situation. How was Nicky supposed to react? It had happened so many times that if she let herself feel anything, it would just end up hurting her. Her mother was emotionally unavailable, and her father wasn't in the picture. How cruel was the world to shove both mommy issues and daddy issues onto her? She sighed as they were on the last legs of their trip to their new "home". Their entire lives had been packed into a single car.

"This is going to be really good for us, baby," Elizabeth said, "We'll be safe here. There's a lot of good people around here, and we're only forty minutes away from your school. Everything's going to be okay."

"I hope so, mom. I hope so. I'm so tired of never settling down," Nicky admitted.

"I'm sorry that I put you through this," her mother sniffled, "I didn't want to get you involved but you know how it goes. I mean, he chased me around with a gun."

"It's okay. Just… I'm going to be honest with you. You need to be more careful with who you pick as a partner."

"I know. I do know that, but actually implementing that is a little more difficult, you know? It's easy to say that I'll do better but humans are messed up beings and just do whatever even if they know they're not doing the right thing," Elizabeth said.

"Yeah," Nicky said.

It was a nice gesture for her mother to say sorry, but apologies weren't enough anymore. She wouldn't treat her mother badly, though. She wouldn't act out in anger, she promised herself that. Elizabeth was the only person she had left. Despite her drug problem and her bad taste in men, she was still her mother and she wanted the best for her. Maybe this new place really would be for the best.

They pulled up at the main gate of the smallholdings and it opened a few minutes later. Their new home was on a plot of land that had about four other small houses on it, far enough for privacy, but close enough for a sense of community.

Each of the little houses were cute cottage style places, painted in a baby blue hue. They pulled up to a cottage near the far back. It had a porch with two chairs stationed on it and a glass door.

"Alright, baby. Let's get unpacking," Elizabeth said.

They carried some boxes inside and Nicky admired the small cottage. The ceiling was high, with wooden support beams going across. The house was already furnished, with antique wooden furniture and a large sofa. The living room and kitchen were open plan, with two bedrooms that both had ensuite bathrooms. The kitchen was quite big and even had a little breakfast nook. For a last minute find, it really wasn't that bad.

When they made their way back to the car to fetch some more boxes, Nicky saw a man leaning against it. His face lit up when he saw both Elizabeth and Nicky. He was oddly familiar, but she wasn't sure where she knew him from exactly. Elizabeth went up to him and hugged him. She gave him a kiss on the cheek.

He was an older man, maybe thirty or so. His hair was dark, but it was starting to gray, giving him the classic salt and pepper look. He was cleanly shaven, and his features were clean-cut. His eyes were a pale blue. He wasn't an overly tall or buff man, but he looked good. He was a little on the leaner side, but his arms were still well toned. He dressed well, even though it was a Sunday and he probably wasn't going anywhere.

Nicky stood in place, awkwardly admiring the man who had just been kissed on the cheek by her mother. Nicky, deep down, felt an instant attraction to him and she didn't know why. She didn't know him, and he was so much older than her. The taboo nature of it sort of turned her on, though, and she wondered if he lived here too.

When she stepped closer, she remembered him. He had occasionally visited Elizabeth when Nicky was sixteen years old. Nicky felt something for him back then, but she didn't quite understand it. It was a strange connection with him, but she dismissed it as a stupid schoolgirl crush. He was kind and good to both Elizabeth and Nicky. He always offered help, but Elizabeth never accepted it until now.

"Nicky, this is Grayson," Elizabeth said, "Grayson, this is Nicky."

"Well, hello there. It's nice to finally meet you. I've heard a lot about you. I hope you enjoy your stay here. I know you'll come to find it quite charming," he said. He threw a wink in her direction and it melted her from the inside out.

Nicky reached her hand out and shook his, noticing how soft his hands were. His cologne was strong and musky, but it wasn't overpowering.

"Grayson is the owner of this plot of land and has graciously let us move in here on such short notice. He lives right there," Elizabeth said. She pointed to a slightly bigger cottage with more modern finishes right next to theirs.

"Oh, thank you for helping us," Nicky said. She felt her knees weaken and nearly buckle beneath her weight. Nicky tried to distract herself from her deviant thoughts by going to grab another box from the car. She knew it wasn't appropriate for her to be feeling the things she was feeling but he was just so damn sexy. Nicky wasn't really sure what her type was because she hadn't quite explored that side of herself yet. Because of her mother's bad luck with men, she kind of steered clear of boys in school, since she was scared she would make the same mistakes as her mother.

But Grayson, with his tattooed forearms and toned arms, Grayson really piqued her interest. She had never felt this way about *anyone* before. She had never looked at someone for the first time and wanted to fuck them so badly, let alone at all. For a long time, she was worried that there was something wrong with her because she never really had crushes on anyone growing up. Maybe she was just going crazy, though.

Grayson helped them carry the rest of their stuff inside. Him and Elizabeth chatted and laughed, but kept their distance. Nicky wasn't really that good with people and wasn't even sure how to broach the prospect of even speaking to him. She wasn't sure what she would say. She kept to herself and unpacked her things. Was this going to be one of her mother's new boyfriends? She hoped not…

Nicky finally exited her room after unpacking most of her stuff. She was hungry now and needed something to drink. Grayson was standing at the breakfast nook, drinking a beer. She stopped in her tracks and stared at him for a while. She didn't know how to deal with the uncontrollable throbbing in her crotch and as she came closer and closer to him, it intensified.

"Your mom's just out… buying some stuff so she asked if I could stay behind and watch you and help you with any unpacking," he said.

"Oh," Nicky breathed, "That's – that's fine."

"Look, Nicky," he looked from left to right before looking at Nicky in the eyes, "I've known your mother for over a decade. I met her before she had you, in fact. I understand that this might be a lot for you right now, so I want you to know that I am here if you need to talk."

"Thank you, Grayson. That's really nice of you, but I am okay, really," she said.

He glared at her a moment before proffering her a sip of his beer. "I know what happened with her last boyfriend and all the boyfriends before him. And your father is even worse. You don't have to bottle everything inside anymore. I convinced your mother to come here so both of you could have a safe place to just be. She means well, despite her fuck ups and I hope that she can get her shit together, for your sake."

She took a long, deep gulp of beer, nearly finishing half of it in one go. "Okay, you got me there. I just put my walls up, you know? I don't have anyone but my mother. Sometimes we can have open honesty between us, but that's only when she's not high on those chemicals. But she's high on those chemicals ninety percent of the time, and the other ten percent, she's coming down and she's hell to be around. It's just an endless cycle of her being a shell of a person and it kills me."

"I'm sorry to hear that, sweetheart. It's good you're here," Grayson said. Nicky took a step over to him and stood close enough to feel his body heat. "I'm sorry you've been dealt this hand in life. It sucks hearing this, but everything's going to be okay and I am here for you. I live right there, you just give me a shout. I'll be around all day most of the time. I work from home."

"Thank you for the offer, and thanks for listening to me. I hope my mom is okay soon, too. I'm kind of banking on it. I don't want to lose her to that stuff," Nicky said. By now, the beer bottle was already empty. She decided to change the subject, she was over the self-pitying conversation. "What do you do?"

"I do remote IT work. Mostly contract work, not really bound to any said company for long, but I prefer it that way. Don't like to be a rat keeping the wheel running for a company that's going to suck out my soul," all the while he spoke, he didn't break eye contact with her, "My second job, really, is well, this plot of land. Managing it, keeping it clean and safe and keeping the riff raff out."

"Wow. That's quite impressive. How did you get this piece of land? Did you inherit it or something?" she said. Her nerves from earlier had dissipated, something she wasn't used to. Usually, every time she spoke to any person that wasn't her mother, she'd be nervous and out of things to talk about within the first minute. With Grayson, though, it flowed like a waterfall and she didn't want it to end. He handed her another beer because he could tell she needed it.

"No, most people just assume that or don't even ask. I actually saved up over five years to buy this plot of land. Then another five to build all these little houses. Designed most of them myself, but got other people to build them, though. I'm not a jack of all trades," he chuckled. He nervously scratched the back of his neck.

His hand was firmly placed on the table. Without realizing, Nicky's hand was near his, and she brushed her pinky finger against his. When he didn't pull away from her touch, she didn't either. It came so naturally for her to move her fingers over his, and lace them between each other. She could tell he was holding his breath by his face going slightly red.

He moved his hand away to take a sip of beer. The tension in the air was heavy and thick and she could have sworn she could touch it and grab it and feel it in between her fingertips.

"So, do you have any plans for after school? You're on your last year now, right?" he asked. His voice was slightly shaky, and she couldn't help but smile at him for it.

"How do you know so much about me?" she teased, "Are you stalking me, or something?"

"I only know what your mother has told me…"

"I'm just busting your balls, silly. Yeah, I'm eighteen and in my last year of school. Honestly, I'm probably going to get some shitty part time job and have a sort of gap year before I get to college," she said.

"Why the gap year, hun?" he said. The more she spoke to him the more things about him she found attractive. His voice was deep. His smile was big. He had a small dimple on the right side of his cheek when he smiled extra wide.

"I've been struggling and fighting and running my entire schooling career, thanks to mom. I've had to study and do homework and exams and everything all the while being in toxic situations. I'm...I'm tired. Also, how stupid is it that I have to do twelve years of schooling only to immediately go into a possible four to seven years, depending on what I choose," Nicky said. She'd never opened up to anyone like this before. It was unfamiliar to her, but it tasted so sweet.

"I completely agree, Nicky. It's twelve years of school, up to an additional seven or more, and then it's off to job hunting. You find a job, you start in the low ranks, and over decades, you build yourself up in that field, but you'll never get that promotion that you are truly hoping for. While you do that, you have to hope that you find love and settle down and have a lovely marriage with kids. You have no time for yourself anymore and you become a shell of a person," he said. His deeply insightful words caught her off guard but attracted her too.

"Oh, man. I feel ya on that one. It's honestly so depressing to me. School. Study. Work. Marriage. Kids. You know, the other reason I'm hesitant to start studying is because I don't actually know what I want to do with my life. How can I make such a major life choice at only eighteen, you know? What also scares me is that even if I get that new shiny degree, I'm not guaranteed a job in that field and it could all end up amounting to nothing and all be a waste of time."

"Yeah, I understand that. It's scary, that's for sure. But it's also exciting and you have so much to look forward to. You've already gotten through everything and came out strong, you can do the rest easily," he said. He smiled at her and she nearly fainted.

"Thank you for the words of encouragement, Gray," she said.

"Of course. Anything to help... You're a lovely young lady. I'm glad that we could meet again," he admitted.

"Me too," Nicky said softly, "I – I missed you."

They were interrupted by her mother loudly opening the front door and coming into the house. Grayson broke eye contact with Nicky for the first time in what felt like hours. Nicky quickly put the beer bottle down and went back to the fridge and pretended to be busy with something else. They hadn't even done anything inappropriate, but they separated from each other as if they had.

Their conversation was normal, but she felt that if her mother had listened in on it, it wouldn't have been good. Although she could sense a bit of tension between him and her, she wasn't sure if he felt the same or not. Maybe she was just going crazy. Maybe all the stress had gotten to her and she was grasping at something that didn't exist just because she needed a sense of comfort.

Elizabeth came into the house carrying a few grocery bags. Nicky looked at her face and knew instantly, that it wasn't just a shopping trip that she had gone out for. She had just bought and used drugs too.

Nicky kept quiet and prepared herself some food. She wasn't going to say anything. Each day that went by her and her mother were drifting apart, and she feared that if she said anything to her, it would further drive a wedge into their relationship.

Nicky went through the motions of life, got ready for school the next day, did homework and everything, while her mother went slightly off the rails. She did job hunting and within a month, somehow landed herself a job in marketing near their new home. More time went by and it seemed like Elizabeth had finally gotten a handle on herself. Nicky grew accustomed to their new environment, out of the city just enough for comfort.

Grayson hung around occasionally and had dinner with them. Elizabeth would flirt with him, and although he would reciprocate it, he would sneak glances at Nicky when her mother wasn't looking. The more and more time they spent together, the more she was attracted to him. He was an intelligent and most importantly kind man and she just wished that they could spend some time alone together to get to know each other better.

One day, she had gotten exactly what she wanted when her mother came to her.

"Hey, baby," Elizabeth said, "Can we talk for a minute?"

"Yeah, of course," Nicky said and put down what she was doing.

"Okay, so, since I've been working so hard at this new place, I've been kind of promoted, if you can call it that. They're going to be giving me my new office and everything and my position will no longer be part time," Elizabeth said. She smiled as she spoke with her hands.

"Wow! Mama, that's amazing!" Nicky said. She got up and hugged her mother, "That's so great. You've come such a long way and you're doing so well. I'm proud of you."

Nicky always felt that she had to be an adult for most of her teenage years. She would have to look after her parents because of their crippling addictions and make sure that they were fed and had enough sleep. She had to be responsible and manage the house. She had to make big decisions that neither her mother nor father could. For once, Nicky felt a sense of relief. Her mother had finally gotten her shit together. She wasn't using as much anymore. Although, some weekends she would snort a few lines, she wouldn't do it during the week. It was an improvement, nonetheless, and Nicky needed to be grateful for everything that came her way. Things were looking up for both of them.

"Thank you, baby. I couldn't have done it without your support," Elizabeth said, "Look, since my hours are going to be increasing from now on, I can't fetch you from school on time."

"Oh," Nicky said, "What are we going to do then? I don't want to sit around at school for hours and wait to be picked up."

"Of course. That's why I was thinking, would you mind if Grayson picked you up from school? Some mornings he will have to take you, too, when I'm especially busy and need to get to the office earlier. Would you be okay with that?"

"Uhm…" Nicky hesitated. She washed over with many confusing, conflicting feelings, "What time would you finish work?"

"I'll usually finish between six and seven but that's really late. If you're not comfortable with Grayson, I'll understand, since you don't know him that well. I can try to organize for a transport service to pick you up or something?" Elizabeth said.

"No, no. That won't be necessary. I'm sure it'll be fine. I guess it's time to get to know him. You've been friends with him for longer than I've been alive, I'm sure I can trust him, right?" Nicky said. She pretended to be hesitant to be alone with him, so her mother didn't suspect a thing. She knew that it was manipulative, but she didn't care. Grayson had been on her mind every single day since they arrived at the cottage for the first time.

"Great, baby! Thank you for understanding and working with me. I told you that we're going to be okay," Elizabeth said. She tucked a tuft of Nicky's hair behind her ear.

"You were right. Everything is going to be more than okay."

When her mother left, Nicky hugged her pillow and screamed into it with excitement. She was eager to spend more time with him and she couldn't wait for it. She was nervous, too. They hadn't been alone together before… What if she made a fool of herself? The next day, she got ready for school but put in extra effort to make herself look nice. She put on some expensive perfume that her mother had bought her years before. She put on her best dress that was still suitable for wearing at school. A white dress that was tight around the bust and flowed down freely from there. She went through the whole day anticipating his arrival.

At the end of the day, she heard the familiar rumbling of his muscle car. She walked up to his car, her heart racing out of her chest. He waved as she came near his car and she waved back. When she got in the car, he looked at her with a cute smile.

"You look nice today," he said, "What's the occasion?"

"Do you want my honest answer, or do you want the appropriate one, Gray?" she asked.

"Are you saying the honest answer is inappropriate? What about both?" he said. He gripped the steering wheel before bringing the engine to life. He pulled into the road and took a different route than she was used to.

"The honest answer isn't appropriate whatsoever, and if anyone else knew, they'd judge me," she played with the long hair of her ponytail as she spoke, "The appropriate answer is that I just dressed for myself today."

"But you didn't tell me the true answer, then," he said. He glanced over at her as they came to a stop. His eyes lingered on her body for far too long for her to think that he didn't feel the same way.

"I got dressed up for you, Gray."

He cleared his throat.

"Why?" he asked.

"Because. I just wanted to look nice for you, that's all," she said, "Where are we going, by the way?"

"took the long route home."

"Oh. Why is that now?" she said. She bit her lip. Being so close to him was making her feel hot and heavy.

"This is the first time we're alone together and I don't want it to end," he said.

Nicky fiddled with her hands nervously and stayed silent. She didn't know what to say to that. She had thought up so many fantasies with him and come up with so many conversations she could have with him, but she wasn't expecting him to say that so soon.

He looked over at her with concern in his eyes. "Look, I shouldn't have said that. I shouldn't speak to you like this. I shouldn't say these things to you. It's not right."

"Why is that, though? I'm eighteen, Gray. And I have been for nearly six months. I'm big now and I've been feeling something for you for a long time."

"Please, please don't say that. We can't do this, Nicky. We just can't. Let's not speak about this again, okay?"

"Okay," Nicky's heart sank. She had hoped this day would end differently.

They drove in silence. The quiet in the car with him nearly killed her. When he pulled up to their cottage, he looked over at her again.

"Look, I'm sorry if that hurt you, but you need to understand where I'm coming from, okay? Your mother and I have been friends for a long time. It wouldn't be right for me to act on my feelings. She's got feelings for me too, you know? It's put me into a very uncomfortable situation because I don't... I don't like her the same way I do you. How would she react if she found out how I felt? She'd fall off the rails again and I would be to blame for it," Grayson opened up.

"So, you do feel the same way, then? Why should you have to limit yourself because of her? Her feelings aren't your problem. Besides, my mother... she might be flirting with you because she wants to keep you around, you know? It might sound a little harsh, but excluding her bad taste in men, she has a penchant to use sex and attraction to get what she wants. Maybe she's just acting this way because you've helped us, and she doesn't know how else to thank you."

"Well, when you put it like that, it makes sense. I wouldn't put it past her. She's a strange woman. Thinking a little deeper, I can definitely see her doing that. You're right. I'm sorry, this is just all so much to process," Gray said.

"She won't ever know, if we don't tell her," Nicky said. They both looked ahead of them and not at each other as they spoke.

"Mmmm," he said.

His hands still tightly gripped the steering wheel, and she admired his arms. She noticed a small tattoo of a little mushroom on his arm. It looked older, as it had bled a little bit over time.

"What's that tattoo about?" She ran a finger over it, feeling the slight bulges of the fine ink lines in his flesh.

"Oh, wow. Had that since I was fifteen, actually," he said. He looked at her for the first time in an hour. "I was a dumb teenager, and I gave that to myself. Stick and poke, I think they call it these days."

"Why a mushroom?" she asked.

"Magic mushrooms were a big thing back in those days," he chuckled nervously, "I was just trying to pull the classic rebellious teenager move."

"That's really cute, actually," she said, "I like it. It's got history."

"You should go inside before I do anything I shouldn't do," he said. His jaw clenched and twitched.

Nicky looked at the time. It was only 4:00 p.m. and her mother wouldn't be home for a while.

"Well, I don't like being alone in that house. Would you at least have lunch with me?" Nicky pleaded.

"I…" he sighed, "Something makes it impossible for me to say no to you. You enchant me, Nicky."

"That's one of the best things I've ever heard anyone say to me," Nicky said, "Wow. Should we go inside then?"

He nodded and walked with her into the cottage. Nicky closed all the curtains of the cottage and went to the kitchen.

"I'll make lunch," he insisted, "I don't mind."

"If you insist."

He made lunch for them. He was quite the cook, and the food ended up being delicious. Nicky and Gray spoke of everything and nothing, except for their conversation in the car. It was as if it hadn't even happened at all. One thing led to another, and they sat on the sofa together and watched TV. He hadn't left immediately after lunch as he had initially planned to do.

They watched some bad drama television shows that were already on when they turned the TV on. She didn't pay attention to it at all as she sneaked him quick glances occasionally. Nicky wanted for him to be looking back at her each time she did, but he wasn't. He sat up pin straight and stared dead ahead, as though he were trying his best to ignore her.

She finally had enough and scooched closer to him. He cleared his throat when her thigh came close to his. Nicky took her eyes off of the television and put her full attention on him. They were finally alone together after all these months and it was about time she got what she wanted. He seemed hesitant, but she didn't care. He had confessed that he wanted her too, so she couldn't wait any longer. She just needed to take the first step because she knew he wasn't going to.

She first started with a touch of his knee. He froze in place as she ran her hand up his thigh, stopping just before his crotch. His jaw clenched again. She stopped herself from giggling. She carried on and touched his crotch, delicately running her fingers over his member. She could have sworn that he was already hard, or he was just so big…

She stroked his length through his pants. His chest rose and fell rapidly. She sat on her knees next to him and put her hand on his cheek. She pulled his face towards hers and touched his lips. They were soft and plump just like a rosebud. They exchanged deep gazes with one another. An intense throbbing in her crotch drove her to press her lips against his.

He didn't kiss back as she had anticipated. They didn't rub back against hers, so she stopped kissing him.

"What's wrong?" she asked.

"Nothing. I mean, we should stop. We shouldn't do this," he said.

He softly shoved her out of the way and stood up.

"But you want me," she said.

"Yes. That's exactly the problem, Nicky. I want you, Nicky. I think about you every fucking day, but I hate myself for it. It's wrong and I shouldn't be making you do this," he said. He rubbed his hands over his face and started walking off. Nicky followed him, but he stepped away from her. They went in sort of a loop, until his back was facing the sofa again.

"You shouldn't be so sure that it's wrong. We're both adults here, right?" she said.

"Yes. But it's different. It's the power dynamic between us that could be seen as wrong," he confessed, "I don't want this to go wrong because I didn't simply push you away and control myself."

"I'm the one that kissed you first. Just blame me for it all if anyone finds out. Just say I'm a nymphomaniac, okay?" she said. Nicky smiled at him and bit his lip.

"No, this is not happening, Nicky," Gray said.

Nicky shook her head. She could tell he wanted it by the way he looked at her. He was just holding himself back. She pressed against his chest with a flat hand, and gently shoved him backwards. He was dumbfounded as she pushed him backwards and he didn't react. She pushed him a few more times until he stumbled backwards onto the couch with a bounce.

Nicky swung a knee over him and got onto his lap. He blinked at her when she put her arms over his shoulders. She kissed his chin and down his jawline, to his neck. He let out a soft moan as his hands sauntered over to her ass. He rubbed her hips, then tugged at the dress until it fell down her chest. Nicky pulled away to show off her assets to him. His mouth hung open at her dainty bralette. Her nipples peaked through the thin, sheer fabric.

He ran his fingers over her breasts, albeit hesitantly. He touched her nipples, gently tickling them. Nicky let out a soft moan as he moved the fabric out of the way and took her nipple into her mouth, gently suckling on it. Nicky ground her crotch against his, the soft fabric of her panties rubbing against his hard, throbbing length.

All her dreams and fantasies of him were finally coming true and every touch and tug and nibble sent her over the edge. He treated her gently, as though she would break if he were too rough.

She couldn't take it anymore, she wanted him to be inside of her. She was already wet enough. She was ready for him, even if he was big. She wouldn't mind the pain because it would turn into pleasure.

Grayson was overcome with an insurmountable lust for her and his strong arms gripped her and flipped her over onto her back. She giggled when she made impact with the couch. Her panties were soaked, and Grayson noticed this when he fumbled with her crotch. He stroked her clit, seemingly expertly, as if they had already explored each other's body's a thousand times over and he knew exactly how to please her.

He fumbled his cock out of his pants. How big his fist was as he grabbed his cock surprised her. Would she even be able to fit him inside of her? She scooted downwards and spread her legs to allow for easier entry.

Just as he brought his cock close, he stopped in his tracks and looked at her with wide eyes.

"You're not a virgin, are you?" he asked.

"No, no, don't worry about that. I lost my virginity when I was like sixteen to some guy," Nicky admitted.

"Okay, good. Because if you were… I couldn't do that to you," Gray said.

"Shh, stop worrying so much. The concept of virginity is bullshit anyway. Don't let that keep you back," she swallowed, "Fuck me, Gray. I want you to fuck me."

He bent over her and whispered in her ear, "I've been waiting for this moment for a long time."

As he said his last word, he lined his cock up, and shoved it inside of her. At first, there was a sharp pain, but she was washed over with a wave of pleasure throughout all her body. He kissed her as he thrust in and out of her, their tongues dancing together in each other's mouths. Nicky could hardly breath from all the pleasure she was feeling. This was nothing like she had ever experienced before. No man had ever made her feel this way and it was turning out to be better than she expected.

He fiddled with her breasts. He was rougher now as he let his walls down and had his way with her. Nicky accidentally scratched his back in a pleasurable stupor, and it was likely to leave a mark. With each one of her moans and squeals of delight, he would increase intensity and thrust into her harder. He was big and he filled her up nicely, not so much that it would hurt, but enough for it to feel incredible. Nicky never wanted this to end.

She felt the familiar kind of thrusts that would signify that he was close. He grunted with each thrust while he looked deeply into her eyes.

She gasped when she realized what was about to happen. "Don't cum inside of me," she pleaded, "I'm not on birth control."

Out of place and out of character for him, he put her hand over her mouth and came inside of her anyway. Her eyes rolled to the back of her head as he gave her a cream pie. Although she didn't want it just a few seconds ago, it felt incredible. No one had ever come inside of her before. Gray was the first person she had fucked without a condom and she understood why most men and boys didn't want to wear one. It didn't feel remotely the same. There was *nothing* like skin on skin. Grayson was different compared to the boys she'd slept with. They never focused on her clit and they just jack hammered her until they came, without worrying about her pleasure.

Grayson also kissed her a lot, keeping a lot of eye contact, and just his overall thrusting even felt better. It was a level of intimacy that she had never experienced before with anyone else. She started laughing out of sheer ecstasy. She didn't know what to do with herself since she was so overwhelmed with how incredible the experience was.

She heard the sound of a car door closing and keys rattling near the porch. Grayson scrambled to get off of her and get his cock back in his pants, and Nicky ran off to her bedroom and closed the door. She slid down with her back against the door and pulled her dress up so that she wasn't naked anymore.

She heard her mother and Grayson chatting, but it was muffled so she didn't understand what they were saying. Nicky bit her lip as she thought back to what she was doing with Grayson just a few seconds ago. She memorized every single movement, kiss, and thrust. She cemented it in her memory so that she may have it forever.

She didn't wash up after. She let his cum leak out of her and into her panties. It was oddly erotic to be walking around the house knowing that that was their own little secret. He was gone by the time she came out of her room. It was probably for the best, since Nicky wasn't sure she could hide her lustful glances at him for much longer, considering that they had finally done the deed.

She hoped that he wouldn't leave and forget about her like all the other boys she fucked had done. Maybe he just left because he was just as overwhelmed as she was. Nicky realized then why she was so attracted to him. He was everything she had ever needed. He was strong and funny and witty. He enriched her soul and gave her a better reason to get up in the morning. He pushed her to do better and do well in life. He acknowledged her. He paid attention to her. Although she understood how messed up it was, she couldn't help but feel that he filled the black hole inside of her, caused by her lack of a fatherly figure.

She had trouble sleeping that night because she couldn't stop thinking about how they ended things. They didn't even have a moment to catch their breaths and talk about what had happened. She felt turned on every time she thought about it. It was so wrong, so hedonistic and terrible, sneaking around and fucking each other. Them almost getting caught made it even sexier. However, a niggling feeling was eating at her. He had come inside of her despite her protests. This was the first time she had ever been unsafe with sex, a lesson she learned from her own mother. Her mother had her at the young age of nineteen, and she never wanted to make that mistake. First thing, as soon as she could, she needed to speak to Grayson about taking her to get Plan B. The prospect of pregnancy terrified her. Especially since this was the first time they had fucked, and they weren't safe about it.

The next morning, her mother had already left the house by the time she had had a shower and finished getting ready for school. She left a note with some money for lunch. It read:

Hey, baby.

Long, busy day ahead of me. Grayson will take you to school today.

Will see you later. Have a good day!

Love, Mom.

Nicky bit her lip. They could be alone again so soon after yesterday. How much could fate be more on their side? It was still nice and early so she could speak to him about it. They met up in his car and it was silent at first before he turned the car keys. He got out of the car and came back with a gift bag and handed it to her without looking at her.

"What's this, Gray?" Nicky asked.

"A gift. To say sorry," he uttered.

She peaked inside of it. An item of clothing, chocolates, and what looked like jewelry were inside. "I can't accept this. You don't have to give me gifts."

"I feel bad, Nicky. I didn't know what else to do," Grayson said. He looked over at her with deep concern in her eyes.

"Wait, are you saying you regret what happened yesterday?" Her chest hurt at the idea of him regretting what they had done.

"No, no! That's not what I meant. Look, I'm not good at these things, but I am trying to make up for the whole… you know, cream pie thing. I feel bad for doing it even though you said I shouldn't. It wasn't right of me," he said. He frowned at her.

"Yeah, I actually wanted to talk to you about that. We're going to have to go grab some Plan B on the way today. I can't get pregnant, Grayson," Nicky said, "That's why I wanted you to pull out."

"Okay," he sighed deeply and ran his hand over his mouth, "About that. I wanted to explain that to you. I can't have kids anymore. I had a vasectomy after I had my first kid. Something washed over me when you begged me not to, something I've never felt before, in a way. I'm never that rough and I never take things just because I want them with no regard for anyone else. I knew that you were concerned about pregnancy, so I think, since I know that's not possible... I just did it anyway."

"Are you serious?" Nicky exclaimed with a smile, "Oh my god, that's so sexy."

"What?" He was taken aback.

"You just take what you want. I wasn't upset because of that, I was just upset because I was worried about pregnancy. Now that that's out of the way... I feel I'm more attracted to you because there are no consequences to fucking you but having a good time."

Nicky looked from left to right to make sure no one on the plot of land was outside of their cottages yet. It was still early, so she decided to take the gamble. Nicky got onto his lap. He knew what was coming, so he instantly unzipped his pants and pulled out his hard cock.

"Already so hard?" she whispered in his ear, "I haven't even done anything sexy yet."

"Well, Nicky, you're a temptress whether you try to be or not," he said back, "I can't control myself around you." He planted kisses along her neck as he spoke.

Nicky giggled out of sheer joy that she finally got what she wanted. She had Grayson now and she wouldn't let go of him.

Masked Mystery

Desiree was a single woman in her early twenties, and she was wild. She lived a sheltered life growing up and as soon as she had the freedom to be her own person, she went off the rails. Not in the sense of ruining her life and career though, but sexually. As soon as she had enough money for her own apartment, she decided it was time for her to start exploring herself in every way possible. She tried one-night stands and random hookups, but it didn't quite satiate her needs enough. There was something missing and she wasn't satisfied enough.

Desiree wanted to give it a chance, since hookup culture was a mainstream thing, and it was so accessible with the technology of the day. But she just couldn't do it anymore. She lacked connection with these people, so the sex wasn't that great. As well as that, the men she went out with were selfish lovers. They fucked her until they were satisfied. One of them, a particularly scrawny man that she decided to give a chance, didn't even touch her body. He didn't play with her breasts or her butt, he just fucked her and that was that. This was her breaking point, pushing her to find other options to find satisfaction.

There were only so many orgasms she could have on her own with the help of a toy before she became sick of it. Cumming was good and all, but nothing like actually having hot, passionate sex. Desiree couldn't remember the last time she had a good lay. She searched online for options, because all her friends lived in a different state and she didn't necessarily want to talk about something like this over text.

Desiree sat down with a bottle of wine for the task ahead of her. Her inhibitions needed to be a little lower for her to go through with this. She worded what she was looking for a million times over, not getting any results. Until she landed on an erotic forum that had a section for the city she lived in. She scrolled through it, forgetting why she was even there in the first place. She went through countless posts consisting of escorts advertising their services and men looking for quick hookups. She grunted in frustration after hours of searching, until she came upon a post titled Masked Mysteries.

Her interest piqued and she clicked on the post. An image of a woman wearing red lipstick and wearing a full face, black leather mask appeared before her. Masked Mysteries was a club just a few miles away from her. They had a vetting process in which to do a background check on people before allowing them in the club, which was promising to her. In the past, the idea of erotic clubs scared her since she'd be surrounded by sex crazed strangers that she didn't know a thing about. This provided her with a sense of comfort. Not only that, but they also required a recent STD test to be sent through before being allowed in the club.

She let out a curious, 'Mmmm,' and read on. It was a no judgment zone, set up inside an old mansion. It had many different sections for the different types of sexual interests that people could have. From BDSM, to orgies, to couples. The possibilities were endless. There was only one catch, though: everyone had to wear masks that concealed their identities at all times.

She sent her application through without even thinking it through and made a point to make an appointment with her doctor to get the test done. She went to the appointment the next morning and got it all done.

She was in a daze, as if she were possessed by someone else. She always wanted to be sexually explorative, but she never knew she would go to such great lengths for it. She thought sex clubs were only for old and bored people, but from the few snapshots she saw from inside the club, people from all walks of life went there. She waited two weeks for her results from the doctor and kept the papers safe for when her application was accepted to the club. She knew it would be, since she had a squeaky-clean record and had never gotten into any trouble in her life.

***

The day she finally received word back from the club, she practically dropped everything she was doing to take a look at it. Maybe this would be her final sexual awakening. Maybe Masked Mysteries would be good for her.

Dearest Desiree,

We received your application, and we are happy to announce that you have been accepted to be part of Masked Mysteries!

Please remember to send through your STD test results, just attach it back to this email. Find attached some rules and extra info!

We would like to formally invite you to an upcoming event this Saturday. Wear whatever makes you comfortable, but please, bring your mask. You will not be allowed past the gates without it on.

Privacy is of the utmost importance.

Kind regards,

Owner of Masked Mysteries,

Mark

Desiree read through everything and it was common sense things, like don't be violent and a long page on consent. She agreed to it all, scanned her test papers and sent it all through. She couldn't contain her excitement. She just needed to find an outfit as well as a mask to wear. By sheer luck, she had a mask from an old Halloween costume from years back. A matte black rubber mask that covered most of the face, barring the mouth. It had small kitten ears on it, and she was happy to be able to wear it again. It was really cute and sexy, but no other occasion had called for it again.

Saturday came and she slept in a little longer that day. Apparently, the parties could go on for long, so long that they could run on into the early hours of the morning, so she needed the extra sleep. She was used to waking up at 6:00 a.m. every single day.

Desiree dug out an old outfit that she was too scared to wear out. A high waisted, form fitting skirt with a deep slit on the side. She wore a black lace bodysuit underneath, with a plunging neckline that would act as her top. She pulled the skirt over it and found a long red trench coat to hide the outfit underneath. She paired the outfit with a chunky platform pump. She hoped that she would be comfortable as soon as she arrived at the mansion, but she knew she wouldn't be okay with walking out of her apartment block and to her car without covering up.

Lastly, she slipped the mask into her handbag and made the journey to the mansion. It was atop a hill and stood tall and proud. It was dark that night, with no moon in sight, but the property was well lit up and it was inviting.

Before she stopped at the main gate, she put on the mask. She took a deep breath and prepared herself for the night. She would be open to trying new things even if they scared her a little, that was all part of the fun, right? The unknown, the taboo, the unspoken dirty deeds.

"You got this, Desiree," she said to herself, "You are going to have a fun night. Don't let anything hold you back."

She entered the main gates and was met with a valet, who took her car to a parking space. She stood in awe and looked up at the monstrous building before her. It was the biggest home she would have ever entered in her life, which was comical to her, since it would be because of a kink club.

She was greeted at the door by both a man and a woman, wearing a tuxedo and a sexy version of one, respectively. They held trays that had glasses of champagne on them and she grabbed one. The main entrance was extravagant with its crystal chandelier and marble floors. She felt as though she had stepped into a completely different life.

"May I take your coat, miss?" a short but buff man asked. All the servants of the mansion wore leather masks with tall bunny ears protruding from them.

"Oh, right, yes, please," she said, "Thank you." Desiree took the coat off and felt slightly naked in the outfit she was wearing. No one stared at her or judged her though, so that was a good start.

"Of course! Just go straight through. There, you will find the buffet and the lounging area nearby, where people like to hang out and talk and find a match, to take to the respective wing of their choice. The back garden is also for those who want a little peace and quiet. I'm sure you've done all your research, but I like to remind people that all the respective wings of the house have different themes. Near the buffet area, there are a couple pamphlets out on display, just in case you get lost and need some guidance," he said.

"Why, thank you again. That's very helpful. I should be okay. Right? Yeah. I'm going to be just fine," she said aloud, but meant to say to herself.

"First timer, huh?" he asked.

"Heh, yeah. Am I really *that* easy to read?" she chuckled.

"You're nervous. Don't be. This is a safe place. If anyone falls into trouble, a helping hand is nearby. Don't you worry at all about that. Just remember: let go, let loose, and have fun!"

"That's exactly what I needed to hear." She smiled at him.

She walked down to the buffet section, which was fully stocked with all the kinds of food she could dream of. It was glorious. At first, she perused the food and snacked on a few things to help calm her nerves. When she felt she was ready, she headed into the lounging area. She felt she was hugely overdressed for the occasion when she saw what the other women were wearing.

There were various sofas scattered around the large living room, most of them filled with people. Most of the women hardly wore anything at all. Some were just in lingerie, while others wore nipple stickers and a pair of panties. Bodies of all shapes and sizes were scattered all over. Big breasts, small breasts, curvy girls and skinny girls. Desiree felt represented in this room and eased up a little. She knew then, that no one would judge her.

She found a semi empty sofa. It was the only one that wasn't overcrowded. She sat down on the sofa. A tall, burly man sat on the couch next to her. His mask was black with small slits for eyes, not enough to obstruct vision, since it sat firmly against his face. Desiree observed the happenings in the room for a while, watching in awe at people kissing and touching each other's bodies. Some left the room, usually the woman leading the man away. It turned her on to see so many people lusting for each other in one room. It made the air almost thick, she could feel everyone else's accumulated arousal in the air she breathed.

"You're awfully quiet," the man next to her said suddenly. It nearly made her jump out of her skin since she was so zoned out.

"Excuse me?" Desiree said.

"I said, you're awfully quiet. You haven't been mingling with anyone here like everyone else is," he said.

"Neither have you, mister. Just like me, you've been sitting here for about an hour and haven't paid any mind to anyone. I noticed a few girls came up to you, but you turned them away. I'd have fucked the hell out of at least three of them, they were drop dead gorgeous. Model material. Is it your first day?" she said. The added anonymity that the mask gave her, made her feel more confident than usual.

"Yes. I'm guessing it's yours too, then?" he asked.

"Correct," she said. She turned her body to face his. He wore suit pants and a white, clean dress shirt. She noticed a tattoo on his forearm, two ravens intertwined together in fine delicate black ink.

"Well, then. You're just as nervous as I am," he said.

"I'm not nervous. Pfft. You're the nervous one. I'm just taking my time and scoping the place out before, I uh," she paused, "Take some sexy hunk to one of the million bedrooms in this house."

"You haven't looked at any man tonight in a way that makes me think you want to fuck them," he said. His honesty made her smile.

"And you haven't looked at any other women in that way. Wait, does that mean you've just been watching me all this time?" she crossed her arms over her chest, "Ugh. Yeah, I just, honestly, none of them are my type."

"What's your type then, kitten?" he said. She throbbed when he called her kitten, something she never realized she'd find attractive.

"How tall are you?" she asked.

"What's that got to do with my question?" he said. He squinted his green eyes at her.

"Just answer my question, mister."

"Six foot three. And a half," he chuckled and scratched the back of his head. Was he getting flustered? She sensed a tension with him that she had never felt with a man before. Was he into her? Because she definitely was into him. The more she spoke to him, the more she wondered how sexy he looked underneath all those clothes.

"My type's six foot three – *and a half* men with green eyes and black hair. Especially when they have a tattoo of Huginn and Muninn on their arm, and they come to a kink party, wearing fancy clothes, a contrast to the rest of the men here, who quite frankly, are slobbish and not what I expected from the pictures."

He coughed into his hand, seemingly from choking on his spit from inhaling so fast. "Y-you… You want *me*?"

"Yes, mister. I've been watching you, too, and I want you. There's just something about you that draws me to you. Hell, we're both new here, so might as well have a little fun together, right? We can't sit on this sofa all night and watch in jealousy at all the other people having fun without us."

She bit her lip in anticipation for his response.

"Honestly, I'm just surprised you know what the tattoo is. Everyone always asks me why I have two black birds on my arm, and it annoys the shit out of me," he said.

"I went through a really embarrassing Norse mythology phase in high school. I don't really want to get too into it, but it was *bad*," she said.

He looked around the room to see that there were only a few people left. She nodded at him in approval and stood up, extending a hand for him to grab. He took her hand in his and she led him to one of the vanilla rooms. This was the first time they would be together, so she didn't want to shove him straight into say, the BDSM section of the mansion. She definitely didn't want to take him to the orgy wing. Desiree wanted him all to herself. She wasn't going to share him with *anybody.*

They found a vacant room and closed the door behind them. It was a little quieter in here now that the door was closed since the passionate moans and grunts were muted. She had her back to the door and looked at him as he looked around the room. He turned to face her, and he seemed hesitant at first.

"You look great, kitten. I really, really like the style. That's also something that draws me to you. That baby doll goth look makes me rock hard," he said. She played with her raven locks and smiled at me.

"I like everything about you," she said, "Will you kiss me, mister?"

He took a few steps forward. All hesitancy left the room as he rammed his body against hers. She could feel the hardness in his pants pressing against her crotch. His lips slammed against hers, shocking her with its intensity at first before she eased into it. He clasped her hips and ran his fingers underneath the fabric of her skirt. His fingertips touching her bare skin sent shivers down her spine in the best possible way.

He nibbled on her lip gently, before firmly grabbing her ass and lifting her up. She wrapped her legs around his waist and her arms around his neck. Now, her entire body was pressed against his and there was no more space between them. It was an intense closeness, coupled with the incredible kiss they shared, that made her forget about everything else in the world but this moment. Desiree purred in pleasure, like a kitten getting its first drop of milk.

She *almost* felt that just by kissing him, she could reach orgasm. It was confusing and exhilarating for her and she never wanted it to end.

His tongue brushed against her bottom lip, daring her to open her mouth. She did, and parted her lips and ran her tongue along his. They swirled and danced together in each other's mouths, only stopping to breathe when they absolutely had to. The experience was most visceral and nearly ethereal to her. How could kissing a man possibly feel so fucking good?

He secured his grasp on her ass, and walked back a step, before turning over and gently laying her on the ground. He didn't spare a second to have his way with her, he didn't care to go to the bed or to the love seat on the side of the room. He wanted her now and she knew it. It intensified it all for her, for a man that she didn't know, to be lusting after her so much that he couldn't wait any more. The man she had only met a few hours before, made her feel more wanted and sexier than any of her past lovers combined. He kissed her some more, his lips gliding against hers.

Desiree took on the arduous task of unbuttoning his white shirt and once the final button was down, she tugged it down his shoulders. He sat up and helped her remove it, their kiss breaking for the first time in what felt like an eternity. Desiree panted heavily from the lack of breathing, but stopped breathing completely to admire his physique. His muscles were defined and clean cut, but not over the top in the body builder sense. He was perfect in every way.

He kissed her collarbones and down her breasts, down to her stomach and then her hips. When he reached her thighs, subsequently the hemline of her skirt, he lifted it up and out of the way. Her bodysuit clung tightly to her crotch and she felt release when he unbuttoned it. The fabric sprung out of the way upon release from said pressure and she let out a little giggle. He groaned when he admired the neatly trimmed bush on her pubic bone, her labia cleanly shaven.

"You have such a pretty pussy," he said. He left little kisses along her crotch.

He waited not a second before diving into her wanting cunt, licking her clit while he reached his hands up above him and explored her body. He touched her waist, her breasts, everything he could fondle while he pleasured her with his mouth.

Desiree moaned and shook and convulsed under his touch. She bit her lip hard before grabbing a fistful of his hair and guided his tongue up and down her slit. He sucked on her clit softly, a sensation she'd never felt before. She didn't even know this man's name and he hadn't even penetrated her yet, but this was the best lay of her life. Desiree's body twitched and convulsed, her back arched and she let out a loud squeaky moan.

"I'm gonna cum," she screamed, "Oh my god, I'm going to cum."

He chuckled and carried on what he was doing, until she had her release. There was a smile on his face as he emerged from her crotch and brought his face closer to hers. Desiree wanted to kiss him. She wanted to kiss him not only because she was attracted to him, but also because he was the first man that had ever made the effort to make her come with oral sex. She was overwhelmed with excitement that there really, truly were good sexual partners out there in the world. One just needed to look…

He kissed her and tasted herself in his mouth.

Against his lips, she whispered: "Will you fuck me, mister?"

"Can I do whatever I want with you, kitten?" he asked.

She nodded enthusiastically, anticipating what he would do. "Yes."

"If you don't like something, tell me. Don't stay silent," he said.

"Yes, Mister."

He kissed her neck again, making butterflies flutter in her stomach. While he did that, he took his cock out of his pants. He placed it firmly against her slit and slid himself inside of her. She gasped at the intensity of pleasure that this stranger's cock gave her. He spread her legs and pulled one up to his chest, her foot daintily dangling in the air. Desiree giggled when he planted kisses on her feet. The masked man was slow and careful while he thrust in and out of her. His slow, steady moves made it feel even better, since she could feel every inch of him inside of her.

Desiree let go of every worry and care in the world and succumbed to the pleasure. She didn't worry to hinder her moans. She was loud and sexy and didn't give a fuck if anyone heard her. She touched his body and he touched hers while they fucked each other. They were so in sync, so in unison that it almost scared her.

He pinned her down and the weight of his body on top of hers was sudden. He kissed her again while he fucked her. It was sloppy and messy and spitty, but neither of them cared. They allowed each other to be free and enjoy themselves.

He trailed his hand up her chest after he pulled away from the kiss, and lightly wrapped his hand around her throat. He nodded at her to ask for approval, and she nodded back. Desiree loved choking, when done right, of course.

He lightly squeezed, adding more and more pressure to get a feel for what she was comfortable with. He looked at her occasionally to gauge where she was at, but she enjoyed it, so he didn't stop. His thrusts grew more and more intense to her while he choked her. Her eyes rolled to the back of her head as her body convulsed again. With a free hand, he rubbed her clit with his thumb and grunted when she arched her back and reached climax.

She lost all feeling in her legs as they shivered uncontrollably. He noticed this, and flipped her over onto her stomach. Satisfied with her satisfaction, he was ready to have his every which way with her. She tried to get on her hands and knees, but he stopped her with a gentle hand shoving her back down flat against the ground. He pushed her legs together and hovered over her.

He licked his hand and rubbed the wet spot against the tip of his cock. Desiree sighed happily when he entered her, but was surprised when he pulled out of her.

Again, with just the tip, he entered her, then pulled out. Over and over. It nearly drove Desiree over the edge. One of the best feelings in the world was when a cock first entered her, and he was doing it *over and over* again. She let out a soft whimper, although it felt great, he was teasing her, and she couldn't take it anymore.

Suddenly, he shoved his entire length inside of her. This position felt great to her, it was oddly different to any other position she had felt before. It felt really, really good. He planted little kisses all over her back as he pumped in and out of her.

Desiree felt incredibly tight and overwhelmed by his size, but she pushed through. The intensity and shocking intimacy of it all made her want to do this forever.

This masked stranger, whose name she didn't even know, who's full face she hadn't even seen, was the best lover she had ever had so far.

He bent over her and she twisted her face to his. They kissed again with eyes closed. He fucked Desiree a little more roughly now, and she loved it just as much as when he was gentle with her. He pulled away quickly, and pulled his cock out of her. He shot cum all over her ass and up her back, some getting in her hair. She turned her head to see the mess he had made and giggled.

"What a big fucking load," she said.

The man struggled to catch his breath, and put a finger up, letting her know that he needed a moment before he could speak. Desiree laid back down and rolled over when he got off of her. They both laid with their backs to the ground, staring up at the ceiling. Their chests took a while to get steady.

He touched the tips of her fingers and she didn't pull away, so he laced his fingers in hers. Still holding his hand, she turned to face him.

"That was incredible," she whispered, "That was the best experience I've had in my life and I don't even know your name."

He chuckled and turned to her. He smiled at her. "Well, that's flattering but I'm sure that's not so true."

"No, I'm being serious, Mister. I've never cum so hard in my life. You're...you're really good. Usually, I don't do this with complete strangers, I at least have a date with them first before I fuck them."

"Today's full of firsts, huh? Yeah. I have never done this before. We just click, I guess. It wasn't my fault it was so good, it was because of our chemistry."

"I'm happy you feel the same way, Mister. Uhm, I don't know how to go about this now. Do we go our separate ways, or? What now?" she asked.

"I have no damn clue, Kitten. Just lay with me," he said. She rested her head on his chest and listened to his heartbeat.

After a while, they prepared to go their separate ways. Before they did, they embraced and shared one last kiss.

"Okay, you don't have to say yes to this if you're not comfortable. Can we do this next week? And the week after? And forever?"

"That sounds good to me, Kitten. Next week. Same time."

The six foot three and a half man came the next week. It was a surprise to her, since she was sort of scared that she would never see him again. She still didn't have his name, nor did she know anything about him. If he never came back, she would never be able to find him again. They had just as much fun as the first night they met. Every week for three months, they saw each other and spent time together until the early hours of the morning. He was strong yet sweet, taking what he wanted but also treating her lovingly and complimenting her body.

Seeing the Masked Mystery every weekend was the only thing she looked forward to anymore. She was addicted to him as a person and addicted to his cock. Her want for the intimacy and passion she felt when she was with him was insatiable. She wouldn't *ever* get enough of him.

One weekend though, she was invited to a family get together. Her aunt, who lived just out of town, was throwing a get together for her daughter's birthday. Desiree was disappointed to see that it fell on a Saturday. She couldn't say no to her aunt. They had been incredibly close to one another since she was a child since Desiree's mother wasn't around much.

Desiree didn't even have his cellphone number so she didn't know how to let him know that she wouldn't be able to make it. It stressed her out to think that maybe another woman would potentially seduce him. She felt territorial over him and wouldn't want him to touch anyone else. She sent an email to the club and decided to ask them to give him a note from her when he arrived at the club, explaining why she couldn't make it.

Desiree got ready for the party. She would arrive a little earlier to help her aunt set up for the party. There would be a lot of people there, so her aunt, Ellen, needed her to help her. Besides, it would be nice to spend time with her again and socialize for the first time in a while. Desiree had been burying her head in her work during the week as well as being fully invested in being with her new sex partner.

Desiree put on a long, flowing summer dress with a flower pattern on it. She put her hair up in a messy bun and put on minimal makeup. She drove to the party and helped her aunt set up. They took tables out from the garage and got some tablecloths and decorations. She helped Ellen ice the birthday cake and set out various condiments for the barbecue. Lastly, they put out some drinks in a cooler. After two hours of set up, they were finished. Desiree greeted people when they arrived, her other aunts and uncles and some cousins.

They fired up the barbecue in the meantime, so everyone could eat as soon as possible. Her cousin, whose birthday it was, hadn't arrived yet. She said that they would be there soon, though. The cousin who was coming, Angelica, was turning thirty years old. Desiree wasn't that close to her, since she had left the house at eighteen and wasn't around much since she had a career of her own.

Desiree socialized and had an overall good time. Until her cousin arrived.

She was latched onto a tall man with dark hair. Desiree was busy filling up some of the snack bowls when she looked up and saw him. Her aunt called her over.

"Des, come 'ere!" Ellen said.

"Sure," she said. She walked over to Angelica and held her breath when she saw the man in front of her. She knew who he was straight away.

"Des, I know you're quite close with my mom, so I wanted to introduce you to my boyfriend, soon to be fiancé, I hope," Angelica giggled.

Desiree's mouth was filled with a sour taste and she felt the veins beating in her forehead.

"Yes, Des, this is Gabriel. Gabriel, this is Desiree," Ellen said.

Desiree meekly put her hand out to shake his. He had gone pale and looked just as sick as she felt. His eyes were wide and so were hers. He shook her hand firmly.

"Nice to meet you, *Gabriel*," she said through gritted teeth.

He had a girlfriend?

And that girlfriend was Angelica!? Desiree felt like she was going to pass out. Angelica was a blonde haired, blue eyed bombshell, who didn't really have that much of a brain. She wasn't smart. She wasn't witty. Her personality was dry, and she was painful to be around. Every time there was a family gathering, she had a different boyfriend. This was due to her being toxic and overall being a terrible person. She would use men for their money, since she was a materialistic person. She would poke and prod at their partners until they broke and left her. Or she would cheat on them to get an easy way out of the relationship. Or that's what Ellen had told her, anyway.

Desiree's heart beat like a drum in her chest. She couldn't fucking believe that he would do this. She felt like a dirty whore for being the woman he cheated on his *almost* fiancé with.

"Nice to meet you, Desiree," he emphasized her name just as she did his. She wasn't expecting this to be how they revealed their identities to one another. She had hoped that it would be a grand thing, and not a stupid mishap like this.

"Oh, he's just great! We've been dating for almost a year now and we couldn't be happier," Angelica looked up at Gabriel, waiting for agreement from him, "Right, honey?"

"Uh, yeah, of course. Of course, everything is amazing on this side!" he said. She could tell he was faking it. From the moment he stepped in front of her, he didn't take his eyes off of her, not even when he was speaking to Ellen or Angelica. She was so conflicted between anger and arousal. Every time she looked at this man or was near him, she wanted to jump on his dick and fuck him.

"Yeah, he's been doing really well at his job too, working super hard! He works weekends a lot these days, though, a lot of late nights! We make it work, though. Hopefully the hard work will pay off," Angelica said. She could tell that Gabriel was miserable in his relationship just by the look in his eye when Angelica gloated about them.

"Oh, that's great! Yeah, I get that. I work weekends a lot these days too. Saturdays are especially hard on me," Desiree said with a smirk.

"Yeah! Exactly. He's home so late on Saturdays, it's like he doesn't want to spend time with me!" Angelica said. It was exactly that kind of passive aggressive behavior in front of other people that ruined every one of Angelica's past relationships.

Gabriel nervously laughed. "Honey, don't say that. I'm working hard for you. Besides, that expensive perfume and those expensive handbags I went into debt for won't pay for themselves."

"Pfft," Angelica scoffed. She seemed to hate him standing up for himself and Desiree found it amusing as hell.

They exchanged some more *pleasantries* before going about the rest of the birthday celebration. The entire time they spoke to people, ate food, and drank, Desiree and Gabriel stared at one another from across the back yard.

Desiree was confused and had no idea how to go about this situation, which was rather sticky. Did she stay quiet or say something? Did she confront him or just go home? It made her even more angry that she saw his face now and it tore her apart. Despite her anger, she was more attracted to him now that she knew who he was and what he looked like.

The party became rather rowdy. Angelica was so self-obsessed that she gathered a crowd around her to boast about her travels and her glamorous life. How could one boast about things they didn't earn for themselves? She fucked men just so they could take her on vacation, especially the Machu Picchu trip she was bragging about right now, she fucked at least three old men to get there.

Desiree seethed as she watched Angelica kiss Gabriel's cheek. He mouthed a 'sorry' in Desiree's direction, but jealousy had overcome her. Desiree had stormed off to keep herself busy with something else, lest she went crazy.

She stormed off to the kitchen and looked through the walk-in grocery closet to find some more crisps for the table outside. The house was quiet, and no one was in the house. Everyone was in the backyard making a noise and busy with their own thing. Desiree wiped away a stray tear. She didn't want to cry, because it was just some meaningless sex, right? What was the point in being upset about him being in a relationship? They didn't know each other, nor did he know her. She should have expected it. She let out a sigh as she stared at the food in the pantry.

"Hey," he said. She jumped in place and held her heart.

"Jesus Christ," Desiree said, "Don't sneak up on me like that."

"Look, please just let me explain myself."

"No. You don't have to. It's fine, I'm not going to judge you. But I'm done. I won't be going to that club again so don't expect me there. I was excited to spend time with you, but I can't do this knowing that you're in a relationship."

"Desiree," he rubbed his hands over his face, "Wow, it's nice saying your name. It suits you by the way. In any case, I don't know if you know anything about Angelica but she's the devil. I've been thinking about leaving her for over six months. That's why I went to Masked Mysteries, Desiree. Because I thought, if I fucked someone else, that would give me a definite reason to leave."

"That doesn't even make sense," Desiree scoffed.

"Let me finish, please. I've tried to end things with her, but she always manipulates me into staying. I'm stuck, Desiree. I don't love her, and she treats me like shit. I didn't mean for things to happen this way. I have been having a really good time with you, and I was going to leave her for you in the end. But I wanted to wait for after her birthday before I did it, okay? I was planning on doing it next weekend. I already have most of my shit packed up. She hasn't even noticed."

"This is too much, Gabriel. I don't know what to say…" Desiree whispered.

"I want you, Desiree. You're drop dead gorgeous and you're a good person. You're smart and you're witty and you're a dork and I love that."

"I…" she started but trailed off.

He approached her and she walked backwards with each step that he took towards her. Before she could utter the rest of her words, he had her pinned against a shelf in the pantry. He closed the door behind them. A string of light streamed through the door, slightly lighting up the small space they were in. She looked up at his green eyes and his chiseled face. His body heat emanated through her dress.

"I'm going to prove that I want you and only you," he purred. He kissed her neck while she fumbled with his pants. She unleashed his cock, and it was already hard. He caressed and squeezed her breasts as she stroked his cock with her delicate, dainty hands. His cock stood tall and proud. He lifted Desiree onto a low overhanging shelf, pushing various food boxes and bags out of the way. She bit her lip, so she didn't make any noise. Knowing that they could be caught at any moment made it all the more tantalizing.

She lined him up and he thrust inside of her. He put his hand over her mouth because he could tell that she was going to moan. She bit onto his hand to stop herself from making any noise. He fucked her roughly and could feel herself getting close from the friction against her pelvic bone. Desiree's eyes rolled to the back of her head, her hands scrambling to find something to grab onto. In the process, she knocked a few things over. As a result, she knocked over an open bag of flour. It landed on the ground and a plume of white smoke exploded into the small space. It messed all over their bodies and clothing.

They chuckled for a few seconds, but were so consumed by lust that they carried on fucking each other. Desiree knocked her head on a shelf behind her head but didn't care about the pain because the pleasure overshadowed it. He closed his eyes and his mouth hung open, he moved in to kiss her one last time before he climaxed inside of her.

With three more deep, hard thrusts, he came inside of her. His cock pulsed and twitched inside of her and she was filled with his hotness.

"Oh my god," Gabriel said, "You're such a temptress, Desiree."

"Well, my name *does* mean desire in French," she purred.

When they exited to the pantry, they looked at each other's clothes. They were covered in white from the bag of flour that spilled. They burst out laughing at one another, frantically trying to wipe it off. It didn't come off of their black clothing and would likely be suspicious if they walked back into the party in the backyard.

"What have we done? We can't go back looking like this," Desiree said.

"Christ. They'll know. Despite this," he gestured to his white stained clothes, "We've also been gone for so long that they'll know anyway."

"Let's get the hell outta here then."

"Are you serious?" he asked.

"Did you come in her car or yours?" Desiree asked.

"Hers," he said with a frown on his face.

"Well, come home with me. They won't even see us leaving," Desiree said.

She grabbed his hand and he nodded.

Desiree and Gabriel ran away together, not caring about the consequences of what was to come. They'd deal with the issues that would arise the next day. The rest of the night would be for them and just them.

For once, they didn't fuck when they were alone together. They went out for drinks and chatted. They got to know each other better and Desiree was happy that this was how things turned out.

Drug Me

He was her age, they had been friends since they were in high school and had been inseparable since. They had sex a few times in the past when they both went through a dry spell consecutively. They were good friends despite their occasional sexual relationships, because they had laid out some rules after the first time they fucked. They promised to not pursue a romantic relationship, out of fear that that would ruin the friendship they had with one another.

Emily sipped on her sangria. They were on one of their weekly "friend dates" at his house, where they caught up, watched movies and talked about their struggles. Hunter was a big support system for her, and she appreciated him as a person.

"Did you have a fun weekend, Em? Get up too much?" Hunter asked. He was a handsome man with blonde beach waves and blue eyes. He almost didn't look *real* to her, that's how attractive he was.

"Made a girl cum with two fingers and my tongue," Emily winked at him. She knew he liked hearing about her girl-on-girl experiences, so she made sure to tell him about it as soon as it happened, "Other than that, got drunk and cried a little."

"Were you drinking tequila again? Tequila always makes you cry. Every. Damn. Time," Hunter said. He threw a skewed, cute smile her way.

Emily rolled her eyes sarcastically, "Well, yeah. Fuck, sometimes I hate you for knowing every tiny detail about me."

"Shut up, you love the shit out of me," he winked.

She bit her lip. "I do," she paused to think of a witty comeback to ease the sexual tension in the room, "But you're like a brother to me."

"Eugh, Christ, Emily! You remember that I've fucked you before right? And in the ass, too? Don't ever say you see me like a brother, or else I'll have to throw up on you." He shook his head profusely.

"Shut up! It's just a joke. Fuck," Emily said.

"Speaking of which, how have the sexcapades been going lately?" he asked.

"Don't remind me. God, it's just so boring lately, Hunter. I'm doing shit most people can only fantasize about, but it's never enough," Emily said. She swiped away her bangs that hung into her eyes. Her red hair was soft and shiny, one of Hunter's favorite physical traits about her. Although kids used to make fun of her for it, she grew to love her ginger hair over time as she grew into an adult.

"What do you mean, Em?" Hunter asked. He took a swig of beer. "I've tried everything, but nothing has quite satiated my needs, ya know? I don't know what else to do."

"Have you *really* tried everything?" Hunter asked.

"I guess not."

Emily bit her lip, and thought of her past experiences as they watched a movie together.

Emily tried playing with strangers in public:

Emily went up to a man in public one day, a filthy little secret under her white summer dress. She had a pair of panties with an attached vibrator. A small toy penetrated her, while a separate piece stimulated her clit. It wasn't on unless a button was turned on, though. A small, matte black remote that had a dial to set intensity. She went up to a man that looked about ten years her senior.

"Hello, mister, are you interested in having a little fun?" she asked.

He looked at her, wide eyed before clearing his throat. "I don't have money for that kind of stuff, sorry."

"Oh, god. No! No, that's not what I was doing. I gave you the wrong impression there. Here, take this remote. Turn it on, see what happens," Emily said. She touched his shoulder and felt his muscles.

He took the small remote and felt it in his hand. Slowly, he turned the dial up until it was all the way up. Emily inhaled sharply at the sudden stimulation of her delicate bits. With the toys inside and out of her both vibrating, it was a little overwhelming. He eyed her up and down, and he smirked when he realized what was going on.

He turned it up and down over and over again, trying to fully understand what was happening. He noticed her tense up when he turned it on high, her chest getting flushed from the pressure. In public, he helped her reach orgasm, while they had a conversation about meaningless things to make it seem like nothing raunchy was happening there.

She stroked his cock over his pants, feeling his hardness, and giving him a sly smile. Emily took the remote from his hand, gave him a kiss on the cheek, and turned on her heels to walk away.

"Wait! Miss! Where are you going?" he pleaded.

"I'm done with you, big guy," she turned around to face him but continued walking backwards, "Thanks for the fun."

"Can I get your number, at least!? You can't leave me hanging like that. I've never had anything like this happen to me and I can't just let that go," the man said.

Emily giggled like a schoolgirl, covering her mouth, and ending it by blowing him a kiss.

This one was a little risky, and although it was fun, it still wasn't enough.

So, she tried dominating others:

She bought a full latex dominatrix outfit. She dominated a woman in her thirties once, which was quite the experience. Women were wonderful creatures and deserved to be worshiped, she realized after making the MILF have multiple orgasms. She'd never forget that one. As fun as it was, Emily wanted more. She enjoyed the sense of power over people, but she wanted more. She went to kink clubs and BDSM conventions.

She got fully invested in it. She dominated some of her lovers who were willing to give it a try. She especially loved dominating, bigger and taller men. It was interesting for her, a five-foot three woman with a small, yet curvy frame, to have full control over a "manly man" that drank beer and fixed cars.

It was fun, but it lasted a few months before she gave up on it.

Emily tried pegging men. She cuckolded men, women, and even the husbands of bisexual men. She had threesomes, foursomes and orgies. She dabbled in public sex. She even tried being dominated herself.

They were all great, yet still not good enough.

So, she would be off to try and chase down the next best thrilling thing to do.

Every time she tried something new, she crossed it out of her notebook, adding onto the failures. Emily had never felt any true orgasm in her whole life. She had come, of course, but she never experienced the satisfying release that other women had when experiencing climax. Every time she finished having fun with someone in a new and exciting way, a little voice in the back of her head would tell her: "Not good enough. Something's missing." The spark just wasn't *there*. She never felt fully satisfied, so now, at the age of twenty-seven, she wasn't sure if she would ever have what she wanted. She was just about ready to give up. She kept this to herself and it was her own personal struggle.

Emily looked over at him after the movie had ended and wondered if it was time to confess her problem to him. Would he even understand?

"Hunter," Emily said, "Can I talk to you?"

"What's up, firecrotch?" he winked.

She playfully smacked his shoulder for that jab. That was her nickname in high school. "This is serious, Hunter. Come on."

"Okay, okay. Fine, I will put my serious hat on." He put an invisible hat on his head and tipped it towards her. She rolled her eyes at him.

"I've never truly felt a full, satisfying climax in my life and I'm kind of stuck with that burden, because I just want to know what it feels like to be completely, truly happy with a sexual experience."

"So you're saying, Em, that all the times we fucked… you were never genuinely satisfied with it? Oof, that hurts," he said.

"No, no. I loved the times we got sexy together, I promise you that. Ugh, I didn't want to make you uncomfortable with this, but I think since we fucked each other before, it's a bit too much of a sensitive subject," Emily said. She nervously twiddled her thumbs as she spoke.

"Sorry. Sorry, Em. I didn't mean to make this about me. Please, speak freely. I'll listen this time," he said.

"Earlier, when I said I've tried everything, I mean it," she listed off the things she had done in the past. His eyes widened, sometimes he would respond with a gasp at especially fucked up or risky things she had partaken in.

"Holy fuck, Emily," Hunter said, "And you just didn't have a good time in the end? Even the foursome with three other girls?"

"Yup. Oh, boy, I can make everyone cum, sure. But I don't know how to explain it, it's like, I'm about to reach orgasm, I feel what it's almost like, like my muscles contracting and stuff, but it just never… goes all the way? I never get the toe curling, eye rolling, Big-O that all women talk about. It's like getting blue balled, I swear. I've spoken to doctors about it and there's nothing *actually* wrong with me," Emily confessed.

He put his hand on her shoulder and rubbed it with his thumb. "I'm so sorry, hun. I really didn't know."

"No, it's fine. I just needed to get it off my chest. There's nothing I can do about it, anyway, right? Might as well just come to accept it and become a catholic nun," Emily joked.

"Well, there is this one thing that you didn't list off. So, I might have an idea for you," Hunter said. He bit his lip and his eyes shifted around the room, as if sifting through his brain.

"At this point, I'll accept anything and everything," Emily said.

"No. Actually, it's not a good idea. Let's drop it," he said. He scratched his head and pursed his lips. He fidgeted with the couch pillow and stopped making eye contact with her.

"Why? How bad could it be?" Emily prodded.

"It just might be a little too fucked up for you and I don't know if you'd be into it. *I am* into it, so if I tell you and you judge me, I'm not sure if things between us would change," he admitted.

"You know I would never judge you. I have probably done much, much worse. We've been through it all, babe. Fuck, I was even there for you when you went through that embarrassing Lord of the Rings phase and it was all you talked about. I'm still here, babe. Tell me. Firstly, I don't want you to feel ashamed and secondly, I'm really, really curious now."

He let out a deep sigh and closed his eyes. "Okay, Emily. Just, hear me out and don't interrupt. I have this kink, right. I've had it for a long time, and I don't know where it came from. I don't necessarily *need* it to get off, I just derive great pleasure from it. I've spoken to ex-girlfriends about it in the past but most of them packed their shit the next day and never looked back when I tried talking about the prospect of trying it out."

"It's not...coprophilia, is it?" she contorted her face in disgust.

"Fuck no, that's disgusting," he said, "I don't know if there's a name for what I specifically like. I've done tons of research online, though, so I know that both men and women love playing into this fantasy and I'm not crazy. I know how to do it safely and I know what to do if anything goes wrong. Girls don't like it because of the risk it involves," he said.

"How bad could it be, Hunter?" she asked. She was concerned, now. What could he be into that would involve so many risks and require so much research?

"I have a fetish called Free Use," he said.

"That's not so bad, hun. Why were you so scared of telling me that? I've heard of it before, but I've never tried it because the opportunity never really came around for it. It's the kind where the guy fucks a girl while she doesn't really react or pay attention to him, right? I'd be into it if you want to," Emily said. She gave him an encouraging smile.

"No, I'm not done yet," he took a deep breath.

She motioned for him to go on.

"I have a kink specifically for drugging a girl and having my way with her," he looked away in shame, "And no, I would never do this to anyone without their consent. I guarantee you that, Emily. I'm not a rapist and you know I would never do something like that. I couldn't do it unless I had a definite yes from someone beforehand, with a lot of planning and preparation. I don't know why I like it, I only ever had one girl give it a shot, but we never really spoke again after a few months of dating."

"I believe you, Hunter. You don't have to justify yourself like that. I know you're not some creep," Emily said. She gave him a comforting squeeze of the hand. "Please, don't be ashamed of your interests."

"The girl I did it with just wanted to do it at the house which was kind of awkward while I waited for her to fall asleep so I could you know, fuck her," he said, "What I haven't tried, which is my ultimate fantasy, is drugging a girl at a bar or club and taking her home with me. If you're not comfortable with it starting out in public, we can figure something else out. Like have it be a house party or something.

That's also part of the fantasy, having other people around first until I can be alone with you and have my way."

"Oh, my," Emily purred. She felt an intense heat all through her skin and body. It was taboo, sure, but it intrigued her. The idea was fun to play around with in her head. She pictured him fucking her while she was unconscious. Her limp body receiving pleasure without him even knowing it.

"You hate me now, don't you?" he said.

"No, Hunter. This sounds pretty amazing, if I'm honest. I'd be down for this," she said enthusiastically.

"Phew," he breathed a sigh of relief, "Good to know you don't think I'm a psychopath."

"Nah, not at all. The thought of it turns me on, actually. You know, I'm pretty turned on just thinking about it."

"I'm already rock-hard thinking about having my way with you, Emily," he said.

"There's only one condition, though. Since I might not be conscious for a lot of it, I want you to record it so I can look back at it later. Is that fair?" she said.

"Fuck yes! I have that really good camera just collecting dust. It'll be good to take it out and actually use it again. Okay, deal."

They discussed the ins and outs of it and laid out some rules and no-nos. He told her he would be careful, but he would have everything prepared in case anything went wrong. Emily wasn't worried, though, because she trusted him. He had told her that he couldn't do it with someone he didn't have a deep connection with, which she understood. It wouldn't be the same with a woman he'd only known for a few weeks or months.

Hunter and Emily went to a dingy pub out of town that no one would recognize them in. They arrived separately, a few minutes apart. Emily had thought about what they would do today, and she preferred to make a big spectacle of it. She wanted to turn it into a fantasy situation of them pretending to not know each other at first to make it extra fun. She got more and more into the fantasy when they spoke about it. Deep down, it sounded sexy to her, most importantly, it sounded exciting.

She wore an extra skimpy outfit for the night, a short wrap around skirt and a tight tank top, with some tall heels. As she entered the bar, she noticed nearly every man that was alone lay their eyes on her. They followed her all throughout the pub as she made her way to the bar and sat on the bar stool. Emily smiled down at herself. She loved the attention. She loved being looked at like a piece of meat.

It made Emily feel desired and sexy. Emily had a bit of a sexual awakening as soon as she turned twenty-one years old. She stopped wearing baggy clothing to hide her body. She went to the gym, not to lose weight, but to feel good *and* look good. Emily got her shit together and started looking after herself, so her confidence went through the roof. She wore whatever made her feel sexy and secure in herself. It just sucked that she didn't receive the sexual satisfaction she was anticipating.

She hoped that this would be it. That maybe, this was just the thing she needed.

Hunter arrived. He wore a white shirt and a black leather jacket, paired with blue jeans. He looked alluring. If he was really a stranger, she would have tried to get his number by now. They exchanged cheeky glances every now and then. When she finished her first warm, bitter bear, he called her over. He had two drinks in his hand, one for him and one for her.

She bit her lip and smiled at him. Emily sauntered over to him and sat on the stool right next to his. They sat facing each other, so their knees would touch. Emily moved a little closer, so that her knee was between his legs and she could touch his crotch subtly.

"What's a sexy girl like you doing in a place like this?" he asked, looking around the dimly lit room filled with middle aged men that smelled of cigarettes.

"I could ask you the same thing, big boy," she said. Emily batted her eyelashes at him.

"I guess I'm just here looking for a little fun, and I got really lucky finding you," he said. She was slightly tipsy by now and she was horny. Somehow, she was more attracted to him now than she had ever been. Perhaps it had something to do with the night ahead of them.

They ordered their third drink. When the bartender brought their third drink, he looked at her.

"Are you ready, Em?" he asked. His face was serious. "I just want to be sure that you really want to do this."

"Yes, Hunter. I am ready. I want to do this with you," she said. She took his hand and placed it under her skirt, so he could feel her sopping cunt, "Just feel how wet I am. If that's not an answer enough then I don't know what is."

He smiled another big, skewed smile, a sharp canine peeking out from beneath his pink mouth. "Alright then. I'll take good care of you. Thank you for trusting me."

He looked left and right, before dropping a white pill into her beer. He made sure that no one saw it so that they wouldn't get in trouble.

They continued the role-play of having just met each other. Within half an hour, she started feeling dizzy and a little weak in the limbs. He noticed her clumsiness when she put down her beer so hard that liquid jumped out and spilled over the counter.

He kissed her on the lips. It was soft but rough, she loved every millisecond of his lips colliding with hers and that was the last thing she remembered.

Hunter guided the clumsy and loopy Emily out of the bar and put her in the back of his car. It was too difficult to get her to fit in the front seat with her acting so out of it. His cock throbbed, so hard that it hurt underneath the tightness of his jeans while he drove her home. He checked on her occasionally through the rear-view mirror, to be sure that she was okay. She was still awake, but had succumbed to being a bumbling fool by this point.

When he stopped at his apartment, he had to put her arm over her shoulder. She was dipping in and out of consciousness while he guided her into the elevator and took her to his apartment. He set her down gently on the bed and set up the camera. He had two for each angle. He had her Hitachi wand within reach as well as some lube. When everything was prepared, he admired her at first. Her skirt was slightly lifted, revealing her innocent white panties. The straps of her shirt were down and with just a simple tug downwards, her breasts would be revealed.

He took his shirt off and walked towards her, adjusting the boner in his pants. The throbbing was unbearable, so if he didn't get some kind of stimulation, he feared he would explode, and not in the good way. He decided to remove his pants and strip completely naked.

He got onto the bed and crouched down next to her. She seemed like she was asleep by now. He gently fondled her breasts. They were soft and supple. Next, he tugged her shirt down, her breasts bouncing out from the fabric. They fell slightly down opposite sides. He took both of them in his hands and caressed them, rotating and squeezing. He pinched both of her nipples softly at first. There was no response from her though, and he squeezed harder, twisting softly.

She let out a sleepy groan. *Good,* he thought, it was good that she could still feel what was happening to her. His dream of making a girl cum when unconscious would come true. He threw a knee over her and got on his haunches, his cock perfectly between her breasts. He pulled a pillow under her head and propped her head up so that it was at a better angle for him. He opened her mouth and shoved the tip of his cock inside.

He put his hands on her left and right breast, squeezing them together, so they engulfed his cock. He fucked both her tits and her mouth. He grunted and groaned, the pleasure becoming too much for him, so he had to stop. If he didn't, he would come too soon, and the night would be ruined.

He took a few steadying breaths before carrying on. He spread her legs wide and they stayed in place. He lifted her skirt out of the way. The white panties, however, he took between two hands and ripped them apart aggressively, before throwing them aside. He got on his haunches between her legs and entered her. She was so tight that it nearly hurt him, but he pushed on.

His mind raced. He couldn't believe that his fantasy was finally coming to life, not only that, but he would also have video proof of it. He fucked her limp body in various positions, only stopping to change when he felt that he was close. Occasionally, a soft, pleasured moan would escape her plump lips, but she was still asleep. It would catch him off guard, but it turned him on even more.

He took the Hitachi wand to her clit when he felt that he was ready to reach climax. Instantly as the vibe was pressed firmly against her clit, she tightened around him. He moaned as his body was filled with warmth all over. He wanted to see if he could make her cum first though, so he controlled himself.

When he felt her walls pulsating, relaxing, and repeating that action, he held it even tighter against her clit and he thrust into her with a great ferocity. Hunter grunted with each thrust. She arched her back, and let out another soft, purring moan. He couldn't believe that he had actually done it. It was so fucking sexy…

He couldn't take it any longer, and unleashed his load inside of her pulsing cunt.

Hunter cleaned up, put her in some comfortable clothes to sleep in, and tucked her into bed. He edited the video for her viewing the next day, before he got into bed and held her. He fell asleep with the hot redhead in his arms, clinging onto her for dear life.

She slept a total of twelve hours before finally waking up, feeling groggy. He had coffee and a nutritious breakfast ready for her. At first, they were silent, but Hunter's big, dorky smile broke it.

"I didn't know I'd have a sort of hangover," Emily said.

"You'll feel better after some coffee and food, I promise," Hunter said.

"Okay," she said.

"Emily. I think I love you. Thank you for doing this for me," he said.

"I... I love you too, Hunter," she said.

When she felt better, he showed her the video of their fun night together. They watched it together on his forty-nine-inch wall mounted television. At first, Emily didn't know how she felt about it, but as it went on, she couldn't help but notice the intense rush of arousal washing over her. It was glorious.

She started touching herself as she watched her very own porno, and Hunter joined in, stroking his cock too. They spent the entire day fucking each other, watching parts of the video, then pausing to fuck each other. She had finally had one of the best climaxes of her life. She felt like she could finally breathe when she got that final release.